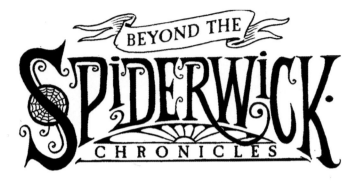

"What do you wish to tell us?"

BEYOND THE SPIDERWICK CHRONICLES

THE WYRM KING

BOOK THREE OF THREE

Tony DiTerlizzi and Holly Black

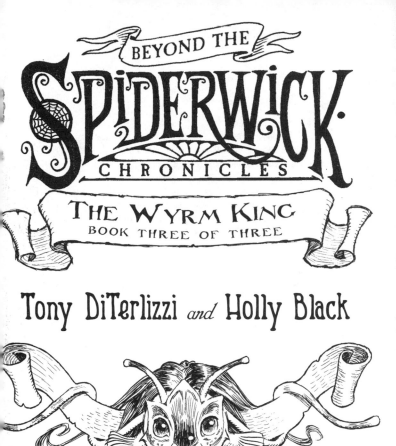

Simon and Schuster Books for Young Readers

New York   London   Toronto   Sydney

SIMON & SCHUSTER BOOKS FOR YOUNG READERS • An imprint of Simon & Schuster Children's Publishing Division • 1230 Avenue of the Americas, New York, New York 10020 • This book is a work of fiction. Any references to historical events, real people, or real locales are used fictitiously. Other names, characters, places, and incidents are products of the author's imagination, and any resemblance to actual events or locales or persons, living or dead, is entirely coincidental. • Copyright © 2009 by Tony DiTerlizzi and Holly Black • All rights reserved, including the right of reproduction in whole or in part in any form. • SIMON & SCHUSTER BOOKS FOR YOUNG READERS is a trademark of Simon & Schuster, Inc. • For information about special discounts for bulk purchases, please contact Simon & Schuster Special Sales at 1-866-506-1949 or business@simonandschuster.com. • The Simon & Schuster Speakers Bureau can bring authors to your live event. For more information or to book an event, contact the Simon & Schuster Speakers Bureau at 1-866-248-3049 or visit our website at www.simonspeakers.com. • Book design by Tony DiTerlizzi and Lizzy Bromley • Manufactured in the United States of America

10 9 8 7 6 5 4 3 2 1

Library of Congress Cataloging-in-Publication Data • DiTerlizzi, Tony. • The wyrm king / Tony DiTerlizzi and Holly Black. — 1st ed. • p. cm. — (Beyond the Spiderwick Chronicles ; [bk. 3]) • Summary: Nick, Jules, Laurie, and their friends try to prevent a hydra from destroying Florida. • ISBN 978-0-689-87133-7 (hardcover : alk. paper) • [1. Hydra (Greek mythology)—Fiction. 2. Giants—Fiction. 3. Brothers and sisters—Fiction. 4. Stepfamilies—Fiction. 5. Magic—Fiction. 6. Florida—Fiction.] I. Black, Holly. II. Title. • PZ7.D629Wor 2009 • [Fic]—dc22 • 2009020723

To my grandfather, Harry,
who liked to make up stories.
—H. B.

To all my friends and family back in Florida.
These images of my old home are for you.
—T. D.

Table of Contents

List of Full-Page Illustrations

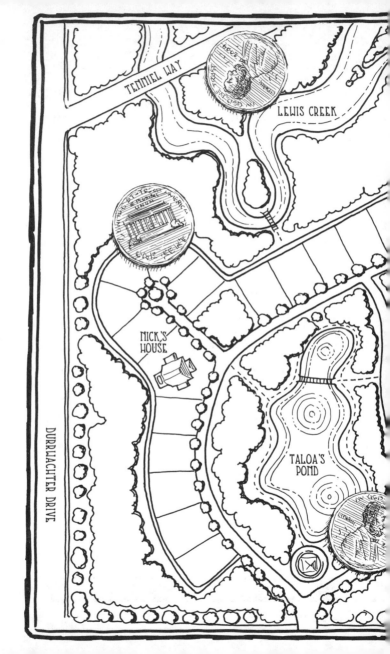

The size of an overturned truck

Chapter One

IN WHICH Nick and Jules Get Their Heads Examined

Nicholas Vargas had imagined a panoply of terrible punishments his dad might impose after he'd stayed out all night with Jules and Laurie. He'd imagined being grounded forever. He'd imagined all future video games and game systems confiscated. He'd imagined being yelled at every day for the next six months.

The actual punishment was much worse. His dad blamed himself for everything.

"This counselor will help us work things

out," Charlene said. She was driving, her hands gripping the wheel too tightly. Nick squirmed next to Jules and Laurie in the backseat. Even though Charlene was wearing sunglasses, Nick could tell her eyes were red and puffy.

His dad also blamed Charlene. The two of them had fought so much that they were basically not speaking. Now they only argued through dark looks and passive-aggressive comments delivered to the air.

The car pulled into the driveway of a small yellow house, where garage doors had been changed out for a wall of windows. Nick could see crystals stuck to the glass, making rainbows dance across the asphalt. It didn't look like a doctor's office at all.

"This person has a degree?" his dad said, making the statement into a question. He appeared to be addressing the windshield.

The inside wasn't much more reassuring. The counselor's office was actually in the converted garage. Soothing instrumental music played in the background. The counselor herself had lots of long silver hair and a few braids secured with silver spirals. She wore jeans. She introduced herself as Teresa Gunnar and told them all to call her by her first name.

DR. GUNNAR

Three big white couches sat opposite a single chair, where Nick guessed Teresa was supposed to sit. On the coffee table rested a box of tissues and a pitcher of water with cucumber slices floating among the ice cubes.

Jules flopped on a couch.

"Let's get started," Teresa said. "We're going to try and maintain positive spiritual energy as we communicate with one another."

They sat down. Nick tried to tune everything out. It was mostly Charlene talking about how his dad hadn't prepared the kids for her and Laurie moving in. Which was true. About how he never talked with them about their grief over their mother's death. Also true. But it didn't matter if those things were true; Nick hated her for saying them.

Looking at the cucumbers bobbing in the water, Nick thought of giants walking along the bottom of the ocean after a slowing, singing boat. He thought of the pages Jared had clutched in his hand, papers that showed there were some kind of wriggly black things worse than giants coming. Jared, the real hero, who would have done the right thing instead of making everything worse. Nick had thought that getting rid of the giants was impossible. Then he'd done it. He'd been really proud of himself too. And, of course, it turned out he shouldn't have gotten rid of them at all.

Which was exactly why he'd started not bothering with anything in the first place — because trying really hard just made you feel terrible when it turned out that all that trying wasn't enough.

"Nick. What are you thinking about?" Teresa asked. "Remember, we're trying to cultivate positive energy and communication."

"Nothing," Nick said, carefully avoiding looking at any of them.

Teresa tapped her pencil against the back of her hand as the silence stretched. "How did you feel about your father remarrying? And what about you, Jules? I'd like to hear from both of you."

"I feel okay," Jules said with a shrug of

his shoulders. "Charlene's nice. And Laurie's cool."

"I didn't like that I had to give up my room," said Nick. He felt like blaming someone for something.

Jules kicked Nick's foot.

"What?" Nick said. "I didn't!"

"Well, *I* didn't mean to take it," Laurie said.

"You didn't care," said Nick.

Jules sighed. "Just until the new house got finished. It was no big deal. Nick's exaggerating."

"So you were angry with your father?" the counselor asked.

"No," Nick said. "I don't know."

"Do you think he's trying to replace your mother?"

Nick looked over at Charlene and Laurie. "I think Dad's trying to be happy."

"That's my fault."

"But not trying to make you happy?"

Nick shook his head. "I didn't say that."

She wrote something on the pad in front of her. "Did you express any of your concerns to your father?"

Nick shrugged.

"That's my fault," said their dad. "I guess with my background—my parents didn't talk things over with me. They were the parents and I just did what they said. That's how things were."

"Dad—," Jules started.

Their father cut him off. "No. I should have talked to you both. I should have seen that you weren't ready for so much change. I know it's my fault that you were acting out—staying out all night, stealing my car. You're good kids. You're not like that."

Nick looked down. "It had nothing to do—"

"Laurie—I know she's a troubled girl." He glanced over at her and shook his head. "I'm sorry—it's just—"

Tears glistened in Laurie's eyes.

"What?" Nick said, turning to his dad. "No, that's not true—"

"Laurie is *not* troubled," Charlene said. She looked at all three of them through narrowed eyes. "Before you start throwing around blame, let me remind you that your seventeen-year-old son kept my very young daughter out all night. What kind of teenager takes little kids out—"

"Have you heard the way your daughter talks? You keep indulging her fantasies of faeries and magic, and what she needs is to be more grounded in the here and now! I know for a fact that they were intently discussing one of her stories that night—"

"So if your kids are so *grounded in the here and now*, how could her story make them do anything—"

"We didn't mean for this to happen." Nick's voice came out louder than he expected.

"No one's mad at you," his dad snapped. "This isn't your fault."

But Nick knew it was his fault. He hadn't been happy about Charlene's moving in. He hadn't liked Laurie at first. And now, even when it was obvious that Laurie was getting blamed for stuff that wasn't her fault, he wasn't saying the right things to fix it.

"We think . . . ," their dad said, and looked over at Charlene. "We think that maybe it would be best for you kids if we separate for a while."

"You can't," Laurie said.

"Dad," Jules said, "Nick and I—we told you we were sorry."

"We've already decided, Jules," Charlene said. "We decided before we came here today. That hotel is a cramped space. It's only making everything worse. We're committed to trying to work things out, but I think we all need a little breathing room."

"Us guys are going to move into a trailer on the build site," their dad said. "We think this is the best thing for everyone."

Nick scooted forward on the couch. "Charlene and Laurie don't have to move out—you guys don't have to move out. We're never going to do anything like that ever again. We totally promise."

"It's done," their dad said. "We're going to give ourselves some time apart. I am considering the matter closed until then, understand? This isn't any of your faults. It's between me and Charlene."

Nick remembered how angry he'd been when Charlene had moved into the house and Laurie had taken his room. He remembered wishing over and over that she'd just go home. He'd made fun of Laurie for believing that things like wishes could come true, but right then Nick had a terrible feeling that she might be right.

Nick looked out the car window at the ocean as they passed over the bridge, this time in his dad's car with all their stuff loaded into the trunk. Boulders remained visible out in the water, like small islands. They looked perfectly normal dotting the horizon until you realized they weren't there a week ago. Until you realized that they were sleeping giants.

On the other side of the bridge, the car veered suddenly to the right, causing Nick's head to bang against the window and then knocking him against the door.

"Why'd you swerve?" he asked.

His dad pulled over onto the shoulder of the road. He was breathing hard. "A sinkhole. Really bad one." He opened the door and stepped out of the car shakily.

Jules pulled his wagon off the road behind them and hopped out.

The sinkhole was a crater in the ground, almost perfectly circular and the size of an overturned truck. Ridges of asphalt ran along the slope that dipped down to a hole. And that pit went so far down that all Nick could see was blackness. He felt a growing sense of dread.

Other cars were edging sharply around it. A few people had stopped to take pictures.

Nick looked over at Jules, who was reaching down to pick up a chunk of road. "Do you think this is it?" he whispered.

Ever since Jared, Simon, and Mallory Grace had shown up with the papers in hand, they'd all known it was only a matter of time before the creatures appeared. They'd taken turns patrolling the beach, looking for evidence. This was definitely evidence.

"Something displaced—pushed out—the dirt underneath," said their father, pressing numbers into his phone. "Probably water.

It happens a lot in Florida. That's why we need the land we build on to be so carefully surveyed. Imagine what happens if a sinkhole forms under a house."

Nick could easily imagine. Too easily.

"Yeah, we're over on Route 1 and there's a big sinkhole," their dad said into the phone. "Oh, really? Huh."

He listened for a few more moments, nodding grimly, then hung up.

"Who was that?" Jules asked as they walked back to their cars.

"I know a guy at city hall," their dad said. "He hadn't heard about this one, but there have been a few others just today."

"A few?" Nick asked.

"Yeah," said their father. "Only locally, but they're spreading."

As his dad's car started to roll forward, Nick

looked back, and for a moment he thought he saw something worming around the edges of the crater, like fingers reaching for a better grip or snakes slithering to the surface.

Debris covered the ground.

Chapter Two

IN WHICH Nick Surprises Himself

Back at the trailer Nick grabbed his dad's computer and logged on. The wireless card that let his father use the Internet when he was scouting for land to develop let Nick get online now. He went over to a news site, looking for articles on sinkholes. He found one, complete with video. When he hit play, he saw a helicopter flying over the southeast coastline of Florida. The vista of ground showed pockmarks dotting the landscape, most of them very close by.

"Put your stuff away," his dad said from the

kitchenette area. He was loading up the mini-fridge with frozen pizza. "This place is too small for us to be making a mess."

Nick swallowed, barely listening. He was staring at the screen. There was no point in pretending he didn't have to handle this. With Noseeum Jack gone and none of the other adults knowing the true cause of the sinkholes, there really was no one else.

He walked over to Jules, who was sitting on a thin mattress and looking through the small duffel of his recovered possessions.

"What's up?" Jules asked. "Find out anything about the hole in the road?"

"Yeah. Can I use your phone?"

Jules handed it over. Nick walked to the window as he dialed. Outside he could see the devastation of the old house and the development. Debris covered the ground—burned timber, concrete rubble, and fluttering plastic tarps. Nick had daydreamed about playing with other kids in the other houses, swimming in the pool, and playing basketball on the courts that hadn't been built. Now he was just dreaming of a world that wasn't about to be destroyed.

Jared picked up on the first ring.

"Are you watching the news?" Nick asked. "You better turn it on."

He heard the television spring to life with the blurring sounds of cop shows and reality shows as someone scrolled through the channels.

"Oh," someone said in the background.

"Let's meet up at Jack's house," Nick said, keeping his voice low. The trailer was small, and he didn't need his father becoming any more suspicious. "I think we need to see the papers again."

"Yeah, okay," said Jared. "But you three are going to have to pick us up."

As Nick clicked off the phone, he realized that Laurie didn't live with them anymore. They couldn't just make up some excuse and all go.

He dialed the number of the Sunpalm Hotel.

"Oh, it's *you*," Laurie said when she got on the line.

"We're going over to Noseeum Jack's house. Everyone. Can you get away?"

"I don't know," she said, still sounding annoyed.

"Something's happening," Nick said.

Her voice changed, turning calm and determined. "Pick me up in ten minutes," she said. "I'll figure out an excuse."

Jules told their dad that he and Nick were going to a junkyard to look for a less mangled bumper for the station wagon. Their dad seemed surprised that Jules was taking Nick along, but he didn't mind. He just warned them to make sure to wear gloves around all that rust. Nick thought tetanus was the least of their worries.

Laurie was quiet in the car. She had fresh red scrapes on her arms that she said were from giving Sandspur a bath. The little faerie was huddled on her lap, licking his toes as if he liked the taste of them. Next to her were Jared, Simon, and Nick, squeezed in pretty tight. Mallory had claimed the front seat after eyeing Jules's clunker with its scrapes and duct-taped bumper suspiciously.

In front of Jack's ramshackle house a sink-hole cut into his lawn. They piled out of the car and went up to the door, which they found locked for the first time in Nick's memory. Mallory slid out her driver's license, ran it through the crack in the door, and pushed the door open.

Her fencing sword clanked on her hip, a sheath tied to two of the belt loops of her cropped cargo pants.

"Did you just break into this house?" Nick asked her.

"Nope," Mallory said, walking inside. "Didn't you see? The door was just open."

Nick gaped at her as they went inside. She seemed like a girl from a video game, the kind who can kick three guys in the chest at once and run in high heels. He had never met anyone like her.

They all settled themselves in the living room, and Jared spread out the pages where they could all see them. Sandspur crawled around on the floor, snatching up palmetto bugs and popping them in his mouth.

Nick frowned at Sandspur and said to Laurie, "Didn't you let him go? We promised we'd let him go."

"I guess he just really likes you guys," said Simon, smiling at Laurie. Simon reached out a finger toward the little creature but pulled it back abruptly when Sandspur bit the air in front of him.

Sandspur opened his mouth in Nick's

direction, showing his red gums. "You promise to feed me. Feed me anything. Feed me until I'm full." He looked at Nick beseechingly with wide, pale eyes.

"You didn't really promise that, did you?" Jared said, turning toward Nick. "They take promises really seriously."

That whole night was a blur. Nick couldn't remember what he'd said. "I don't think so."

"You did. Jules said it. You all promised together," said the faerie.

Laurie didn't look at Nick. "Leave Sandzy alone. Just tell us about the thing you saw."

Nick groaned. "What is your problem?"

"My mom didn't have to spell it out. You didn't want us. That's what you said in therapy, right? You were just too scared to say it to my face."

"No, that's not what—"

"Forget it. We have more important stuff going on." She pointed to the papers.

"Look," Nick said. "We never said we didn't want you!"

"Do you?" Laurie said.

He was silent.

"Did you say that you *want* us to live with you? Did you tell your dad that?"

Nick hadn't said that. Not exactly.

"Yeah," she said, getting up and walking out so that the screen door banged after her, stopping only to call back, "that's what I thought."

Nick started to get up. He didn't want her to be mad at him, but he had no idea how to stop her.

"Hang on," said Mallory. "I don't know what's going on, but let her cool off. Anyway, we need to talk about what you saw."

Nick sighed. "I don't really know what it

was. I thought I saw something crawling up out of the sinkhole. Somethings. Like snakes. Not exactly like the picture, but close enough that I think it must be the thing we're worried about."

"Like this one?" Simon got down on his hands and knees to point to one of the pieces of paper. There was a sketch that looked like a ball of squiggles, with the note "As the rat king is to rats, so the wyrm." Noseeum Jack's father might have been a great researcher, but maybe not such a great artist.

Nick squinted at the drawing. They'd looked at it a dozen times and never known quite what to make of it. "Hard to say."

"How dangerous could a bunch of salamanders be?" Jules asked. "I mean, more dangerous than gnarly, fire-breathing giants? I don't think so."

"Here's what we know," Mallory said, pointing to the pages. "The giants have some kind of natural enemy. Both of them wake up. They fight until they take each other out. And based on this drawing, the giants' natural enemy appears to be an evil ball of yarn."

Jules snorted.

"Snakes or salamanders, I guess," Jared said, tilting his head to look at it from a different angle. "Dragons, maybe. Even if it looks like a bowl of spaghetti. But it's close enough to what Nick saw."

"Here," Nick said, pointing to another piece of paper with an annotation. "I don't think Jack's dad drew this from life. He copied it from somewhere—a legend some settler had been told. Jack's dad wasn't around when it happened the last time. It was five hundred years ago. That's the sixteenth century. Or the fourteenth century. It's fifteen-oh-something. Which way does it go?"

"Dude," Jules said.

"Ponce de León shows up not even ten years after," Nick said, seeing everyone's blank stares. "He was this Spanish explorer. Looking for the fountain of youth."

"I guess someone studies," Mallory said with a pointed look in Jared's direction.

"Whatever," Jared said. "How does Nick's showing off help?"

Nick gave Jared a poisonous look. "I'm not showing off. I'm just saying. He couldn't have drawn this from life."

"Come on," said Jules. "Chill out, you two."

"I didn't think he was showing off," said Simon, patting Nick on the shoulder.

Jared scowled. "What's a rat king, anyway? That's what we need to know."

Simon looked up from the papers. "Oh. I know that. It's crazy. Sometimes when there are a lot of rats in a small space—like during plagues or whatever—then the dirt or blood or, uh, other stuff sticks their tails together. And

they start thinking differently—almost like they're one creature. Isn't that awesome?"

Nick tried to picture it. "That can't be real."

Jared started to laugh. "That's gross."

"There are mummified ones in museums," said Simon, grinning. "Really gross."

"Then they die, right?" Nick asked. "They can't live like that."

Simon shook his head excitedly. "Sometimes one will die and the rat king will just roll on. They can live a long time like that."

"Ugh." Mallory shivered. "Rats freak me out."

"There are reports of

squirrel kings and field mice that got tangled up the same way. And I also heard about all kinds of . . ." Simon stopped as he noticed that everyone else was staring at him. He shrugged his shoulders. "It's kind of cool."

"Hey, what's this?" Jules pointed to a piece of paper that looked like it had been ripped out of an old book—an old engraving of a hydra with a single large body and multiple waving heads. It looked utterly terrifying.

Nick really hoped that that had gotten in among the other pages by accident.

This sinkhole was much larger.

Chapter Three

IN WHICH Someone Familiar Returns as Everything Else Becomes Unfamiliar

As the others continued discussing the wormish, snakish things and how they could cause sinkholes, Nick went outside to find Laurie. Pausing in front of the door, he looked across the front yard at the pit yawning closer to the house. A motorcycle was parked down the street, but he didn't see any other cars. No neighbors, either. He went around the side of the house, heading toward the back.

He didn't see Laurie, just overturned buckets

and some beams leaning against the house, like Jack had been about to do some repairs. Nick's mind wandered to the last time he'd seen Jack and how Jack had told him there was something in the back for him. It had turned out to be an old, scummy kiddie pool. Maybe Laurie had gone there to check on how the mosquito larvae were enjoying breeding in it.

Turning the corner to the backyard, Nick didn't see Laurie, but he saw the pool. Bright blue plastic, covered with images of a grinning fish, and as thick with slime as before.

"Laurie?" he called.

Something moved beneath the green sludge. It was such a subtle shift in the water that he almost doubted he'd really seen it, but Jack had said there was something back here. Maybe there was. Leaning down slowly, Nick picked up a stick and drew it over the water, parting the lily pads and slime. Then he poked deeper.

Nick stumbled back as a head rose. For a moment he thought Laurie had decided to go for the most disgusting swim ever. Then, as the head turned toward him, he saw another head surfacing. And another.

A nixie blinked her golden eyes at him.

"Taloa?"

"*Yes, Nick-la,*" sang another, pushing back the murk and lily pads. Taloa and two of her sisters were here, in Jack's kiddie pool. Nick grinned crazily. That was what Jack had been trying to tell him. *Something you were thinkin' on.*

"You're okay," he said, feeling stupid.

"*We are prisoners la-le-la. The man captured la-le-lo us and brought us la-la-le here.*"

"*Yes,*" sang one of the sisters. "*A bad man la-le-lo-le-la.*"

"Something you were thinkin' on."

"But why?" Nick asked. "Why would Jack bring you here?"

"He wanted us to sing for him," sang Taloa. *"But we wouldn't le-la."*

Sing for him? Had Jack already figured out that they were going to need to lure the giants out to sea? Nick tried to think back, but he couldn't remember Jack knowing anything about their plan. Maybe Jack had a plan of his own. A cold feeling of dread crept up Nick's spine. "How long have you been here?"

"La-le-lo," sang one of the sisters. *"Many days and nights."*

Nick swallowed. The nixies must have been in the pool before Jack left with his son. Before Jack was hurt, certainly, or he wouldn't have been able to carry them here. Which meant that the night when Nick had mentioned Taloa and Jack had said they could deal with it later, Taloa had already been caught and brought here.

"You've been here since you left us the note?" Nick asked numbly.

Taloa blinked several times, quickly, and nodded. *"He said he would show me where my sisters were la-le-lo. I should not have gone with him."*

Nick's head swam.

"You will take us back to the pond le-la?"

"The pond's not safe," Nick said, thinking of the development and the construction that would be coming. "We need to find you a good stream. One where there aren't a lot of people."

"Yes le-la-lo," sang Taloa. *"Bring us to this place."*

Nick wasn't sure where there was an untainted stream or a pristine lake, but he was horrified at the thought of the nixies staying here as the water level continued to drop and the scum got thicker.

Then Laurie walked around the corner of the house, Sandspur resting on her hip. She'd been frowning, but when she saw Taloa, a huge smile spread across her face.

"Tally!" Laurie yelled, continuing her habit of giving unearthly creatures stupid nicknames.

"Laurie la-lo-le!" Taloa seemed glad to see Laurie, which made Nick feel weirdly hurt.

"Hey," Jules shouted from the front yard. "Are you two done fighting? Because we want to go take a look at the sinkhole."

Nick and Laurie exchanged glances. He needed to tell her something that would make her forgive him, but he had no idea what to say. It wasn't fair. Her mother had decided to move out too. It wasn't just his fault.

"We'll be there in a second," he shouted back, stalling for time.

"I don't want to talk to you anyway," Laurie snapped, and turned away from him.

"Good," he said automatically. Then he turned to Taloa. "We'll be right back, and then we'll get you out of here."

Taloa reached out her hand and caught his. Her skin felt damp and cool, and he couldn't stop staring at the way a membrane stretched between her fingers like webbing.

"Don't make me a promise you don't intend to keep le-la," she sang, her voice low and grave.

Right, Nick thought. *Promises.*

This sinkhole was much larger than the one on the highway and looked larger than it had minutes ago. It stretched across the whole road and, in addition to coming close to Jack's house, stretched onto the lawn of another house that looked like it had been abandoned. Even the motorcycle was gone. One of the nearby palm trees sagged dangerously toward the pit. They could see the dirt floor about seven feet down. Nick thought he saw some flickering movement in the shadows.

"Do you think that ground's solid?" Mallory said, peering down at the floor of the sinkhole. "Do sinkholes fall more if you touch the bottom?"

"I don't know," said Jules. "Maybe we could drop something down and see what happens."

"I'll get rope." Mallory walked back in the direction of the house.

Nick crouched down, trying to figure out what he'd seen moving. It might have just been the shadows cast by the tree. He shuffled closer and found himself taking breaths in short, rapid gasps. His pulse raced. There was something odd about the air.

Mallory came back with rope, but she'd tied it around her own waist. Nick stood up, backing away from the pit.

"What are you doing?" Jared asked.

"Wait," Nick said.

"Hold this," Mallory said to Jared. As he grabbed hold of the end of the rope that she handed him, she took three quick steps and jumped into the pit.

"She always does this!" yelled Jared. He braced himself, leaning back. "If there's a stream, she's got to wade into it. If there's an enormous red-capped goblin, she's got to charge it."

"Oh yeah," said Simon, "you're one to talk. If Thimbletack tells you not to do something, what's the first thing you do?"

"She always does this!"

Mallory landed on loose dirt. She looked around and then gave a little gasp.

"What's wrong?" Laurie called down.

Worming out of the ground all around Mallory were snakelike shapes, their heads as craggy and pointed as turtles, their bodies wriggling, their tiny arms digging in the loose dirt. Mallory sprang back to the side of the pit. She began to climb and then slipped. She seemed oddly unsteady.

"Mallory!" Jared yelled.

Losing her hold on the rope, Mallory fell back down on her hands and knees in the dirt. Rustling surrounded her as vague shapes writhed on the ground. Her hands went to her throat. Her mouth opened, but all that came out was a horrible, choking sound.

"Something's wrong with her," Simon said.

"The air," Nick said. "She can't breathe.

There's something wrong with the air."

"Mallory!" Jared screamed. "Climb! Climb!"

Jules grabbed the rope out of Jared's slack hands. "We've got to get her out."

Nick took hold of the rope too.

"Pull!" Jules shouted.

Nick pulled.

Jared snapped out of his daze and started to tug, Simon and Laurie joining in front of him. Jules stepped back, anchoring their efforts. The loop of nylon around Mallory's waist slid up to just under her arms. Her slack body bumped against the wall of the sinkhole as she rose, her sword dragging up the side.

Nick took a deep breath and held it, running forward to try to stuff his shirt between Mallory and the rough ground as they pulled her up over the edge. Already a cut above her eyebrow was oozing blood, there was a rip in her capris, and

"What are these things?"

one of her legs looked badly scraped. Her eyes fluttered open, then closed again.

They managed to carry her onto the soft grass, where she choked and then, crawling to her knees, threw up. Laurie brushed Mallory's hair back from her face. Looking down, Nick saw three glossy black creatures scuttling away from Mallory. Their tails seemed tangled together.

Nick grabbed hold of the creatures' tails and held them up and as far away from him as he could. They snapped at one another in the air and tried to crawl up one another's bodies to Nick's arm.

"Get a jar," he yelled to Simon.

"No, Simon, stay here," Jules said, and raced off himself in the direction of Jack's house.

"Ugh, what are these things?" Nick said, shaking them until they went limp.

Jules came back with two mason jars, one

empty and the other filled with water. He brought the water over to Mallory, who swigged a little, then spat it out. She drank the rest in three swallows.

"You okay?" Jared asked her, his hand on her shoulder.

"I think so," Mallory said.

Then, gingerly, Jules held the empty jar so Nick could drop the creatures inside. Jules slammed the lid down as they began to work their way up the glass. He looked more closely at their tails. They weren't so much knotted together as tangled with dirt and roots, which binded them like glue.

"I couldn't smell anything," Mallory said, gasping. "But I was breathing something that wasn't air. There were lots of those things." She pointed to the jar. "I have no idea what happened."

"Could be methane," Jules said, tilting the jar and watching the creatures scrabble around. "That's odorless."

"Methane," said Simon. "That would make sense. It displaces oxygen."

"It's why you can't build on a landfill," said Jules. Nick looked at him in surprise. Jules rolled his eyes. "Oh, come on, I can't know anything? Dad's a builder."

"Okay," Nick said. "See me acknowledging that you have a brain. What else do we know about methane?"

Jules shrugged. "It's flammable."

"Fire-breathing," said Jared. "Fire-breathing dragons? Could the methane be coming from them? Could they be breathing it out?"

Nick looked at the creatures in the jar. They seemed so small to be so dangerous. Then he imagined all the sinkholes he'd seen online

They seemed so small.

brimming with them and shuddered.

Laurie walked over to look at the creatures too. They scraped tiny claws against the side of the jar. "Well," she said, "I guess now we know what's worse than giants."

"You will take us to a bigger water."

Chapter Four

IN WHICH They Drive in Circles

Loading the nixies into the station wagon was the hardest part. First Jules put down a somewhat shabby tarp, and then Nick covered the back in soaking wet towels. The nixies used several more wet towels as cloaks. They huddled there, singing softly to themselves.

"You will take us to a bigger water la-lo." Taloa's voice was firm.

"We're getting out of here before the sinkhole gets any bigger," Nick said. "We'll figure out a good stream for you, I pro—"

"Don't *promise*," Mallory said. She was leaning on the long wooden handle of a rake and looked pale.

Taloa glared at her with golden eyes.

"We're going to do our best," Mallory said to the nixie, and put her hand on Nick's shoulder. "Come on, get in the car."

Nick sat in the front so that Mallory could slump between her two brothers in the back, with Laurie crushed against the door. Simon wound up stuck with the jar of creepy dragons on his lap and kept glancing at Laurie's lap like he was trying to figure out a way to trade them for Sandspur.

"Maybe we should give them names," Simon said resignedly, tapping the glass.

"No," the rest of the backseat chorused. That made Nick grin, but looking at Mallory's pale, clammy skin made the smile fade fast.

"We should give them names."

"Are you sure you don't want to go to the hospital?" he asked her.

"The next person who mentions the hospital is going to get my fist in their face." She didn't even bother to open her eyes.

It made Nick nervous to see her half asleep like that. It was too similar to seeing her collapsed at the bottom of that pit. Jared must have felt the same way, since he poked her leg with his foot. She opened her eyes enough to look annoyed.

"Okay," Jules said from the front. "Somebody tell me where I'm supposed to be going."

Nick shook his head. "We have to figure out what those things have to do with the sinkholes. And how to stop the sinkholes from spreading. And find a safe stream for the nixies."

Laurie looked over at the jar. "How do you think the tails get tangled like that? Like that rat king thing?"

"Oh," Nick said. "Simon, how big can a rat king get?"

Simon shrugged. "I'm not an expert or anything, but I guess it depends on how many rats. Theoretically? Really big."

Nick thought of the drawing of the hydra with its waving necks and enormous body. He thought of the badly drawn ball of string they'd found among the papers at Jack's house. Lots of horrible little creatures were bad enough, but the idea of their knotting together into some monster made the hair stand up along his arms.

"So what we need to know," said Laurie, "is how many dragon-lizard things are down there."

"Lots," Mallory mumbled.

"Knowing what they are would also be good," put in Jared.

Simon held up the jar. "They look a lot like the salamanders we saw back home."

"You mean the ones that turned out to be baby dragons?" Laurie asked.

Sometimes her knowing practically everything there was to know about faeries had its advantages, Nick thought.

Jared and Simon exchanged a look.

"Look," Nick said. "If there's something you're not telling us because you think we're going to be freaked out, I'm already freaked. I doubt you can make it much worse."

"They do look a little like baby dragons," Simon said. "But the ones we encountered back in Maine were poisonous—just touching them would burn you. See?" He pulled the collar of his shirt wide to show where a scar ran up the side of his neck. "These whatever-they-ares made Mallory pass out, but they didn't burn her."

"See?"

"They didn't burn my fingers, either," Nick said. "You know, when I picked them up."

"So they're not dragons," Laurie said.

"Since none of you have any idea where we're going, I'm stopping for gas," Jules said, and pulled into a station. He got out and leaned back in the window. "You want anything from inside?"

No one did.

As Jules headed for the little market, Simon continued. "Well, they still could be dragons."

"And for a moment we were all reassured," Jared said, moodily pushing black hair off his face. "Thanks, Simon."

"Well, animals look different in different regions. I mean, think about all the different ways that toads look. And how one kind might be bright-colored and poisonous while another kind might be really camouflaged and not poisonous at all." He held up the jar. "So these might be dragons—just not the same kind of dragons we have in Maine."

Jules's phone rang, rattling in the cup holder. Nick picked it up and looked at the number. It was their dad. He clicked the button and put the phone to his ear. "Hello?"

"Jules?" their dad said.

"No." Nick shifted guiltily in his seat, already anticipating having to lie. "It's me, Nick."

"Where are you kids?"

Nick looked around. "Just finished at the junkyard. We didn't find anything good."

"Don't come back to the development. A big sinkhole opened up along the main road. I got the car around it, but it's widening. Tell me what's close and I'll come and meet you."

"Maybe you should go to Charlene's," Nick said. Laurie gave him a dark look from the backseat.

His dad hesitated.

"What if a sinkhole opened by the hotel?" Nick said, hoping that this was the right thing to say. Hoping that if his dad and Charlene could spend some time together without fighting, things could go back to normal. Whatever normal was. "We could meet you there," he added.

"I'll call you from there," his dad said. "Just to let you know I made it. If you're in a safe place, stay where you are until I call. Then we'll meet up. We might have to evacuate. You and your brother be careful, all right, Nicholas? Stay safe."

Nick closed the phone with a sinking heart as Jules got back in the car with two hot dogs and a congealed piece of pizza.

"Who was that?" Jules asked.

"Your dad," Laurie said. "Why did you tell him to go to my mom's?"

"I don't know," Nick said.

"You better figure it out," she said. "You better decide what you want, Nick."

"Hey," Jared said to Jules, "can I have some of the pizza? I want to feed these dragon things something. See what they do."

Jules sighed but handed the piece over.

Simon unscrewed the top of the jar, and Jared dropped a chunk of pizza inside. One of the little mouths bit down on the cheese, and then its torso twisted back so that another head could attack the slice.

"Uh," Nick said.

The tiny creatures were rotating faster, each one tearing off a chunk of food and swallowing it so quickly that it was gone in moments. Their bodies swelled at first, then stretched like worms. When they stopped stretching, they seemed much longer.

"Uh," Nick said again. "I think they're growing."

"That's what animals do," said Simon.

"But I can *see* them growing," said Nick.

"That giant. The first one," Laurie said. "The one that Jack killed. It was looking for salamanders. It was rooting around in the dirt for them."

"So the giants eat the salamander-dragon things, which keeps the population down," said Simon.

"Which explains the papers we found," Jared finished. "So what happens normally? Like if we hadn't interfered, what would have happened?"

"I guess the giants fight with one another by eating the baby dragons and breathing flame. This cuts down the baby dragon population, but also burns down lots of stuff. But if there are no giants, then the dragons turn into hydras and destroy everything. There's nothing to check their destruction. Does that sound about right?" Laurie said. The jar rocked back and forth as each of the dragons battered at the glass, trying to get to where Sandspur was finishing off the rest of the piece of pizza. They were bigger than they had been moments ago, nearly too big for the jar.

"We have to get the giants back to shore," Nick said. "And we have to do it now."

The cap was still in his hand.

Chapter Five

IN WHICH They Go to the Beach

The giants had been drawn out to sea by the mermaid's song, recorded and replayed with amplification thanks to hastily rigged electronics and a model boat. The giants had obediently followed the singing into the water. Maybe singing could bring them back, too.

"Taloa," Nick said, "we need your help."

"What do you want her to do?" Laurie asked, leaning forward in her seat like she could protect the nixies.

"You said la-lo-lee-la you would find us water

la," sang Taloa from the far back of the station wagon.

"We have to go to the beach," Jules said.

"No," sang one of the other sisters.

"What's your name?" Laurie asked. "I'm Laurie."

"Ooki," sang one of the sisters. *"That's what people called me lo-lee before. And my sister has lo-la-ah been called Ibi."*

"We need your help," Nick put in. "Nowhere's safe right now, but maybe we can fix that. Then you could have your pick of streams or rivers or ponds. You could pick anything—"

"Why should we la-le help you?" Taloa sang. *"You never found my la-le-lo sisters la-lee. Your la friend lo-lee kept us prisoners la. I do not trust you."*

"We need you to sing and lure back the giants. They're out in the sea—we're not sure how far out or how many of them we can get back, but we need to. They have to come back and eat all the dragons that are breeding in sinkholes. Um, things are bad now but they're going to get a lot worse. For everyone."

"*No,*" Taloa sang.

"Why not?" Simon asked her.

"*I will not lo-le help Nicholas.*"

Nick stared into her golden eyes and shuddered. "But why not?"

She pointed a webbed finger at him. It reminded him uncomfortably of the mermaids and their cold stares as they dragged Jules underwater. "*You found no sisters lo-le. I owe you la-lo nothing. I am glad la-lee-la the giants are gone.*"

"We have to do something," Nick said. He thought about himself, just a few weeks ago, not bothering with anything. Not thinking he could change things. Now he was afraid that

71

"No helping."

he had changed things too much and didn't know how to change them back. "We have to keep the dragons from getting big enough to destroy everything. Or you'll all be in danger again."

"No giants la-lo-le," sang Taloa. *"No helping."*

"Simon, hold up the jar," Nick said.

Simon raised the jar of large dragon-lizards so that the nixies could peer at them. One of the dragonish things snapped at Ooki.

"These things get tangled together, they grow, and then they eat a lot of stuff. Plus sinkholes are no good for streams. And there are sinkholes opening up all over the place because of these creatures." Nick paused. "If you help us now, I promise I'll take you wherever you want. Any stream. Any lake. Anywhere."

"Do you la-lo swear on your life?" asked Taloa, the nictitating membrane closing over her eyes and then opening again.

He shivered. "Yes."

"You can't keep promising like that," Jared said, aghast.

But Nick had nothing to give anyone but promises.

"I will help," sang Ooki.

"I will help too," sang the other.

"No," Taloa sang. *"Le-lo-le we must hide from the giants. We must not trust the humans further. Even with their la-lo promises."*

"Tell us your plan, Nicholas," sang the sisters, huddled in the light blue towels.

"Do you even have a plan?" Jules asked softly.

Nick shrugged. "Um, get the nixies to sing? Get the giants back? Get out of the way?"

Jules laughed. Laurie and Jared exchanged glances.

"We're going to need to get the nixies out on the water," Jared said. "Even if sound carries over water, they're still going to have to be out far enough to get the giants' attention."

"My sisters lo-le-la do not like la-lo salt," sang Taloa. *"They will not la-lo swim in the sea."*

"We need a boat," said Jared.

"I don't know where we can get a boat," Jules said. "But I know where I can get a surfboard."

The quickest way to get a surfboard was to borrow it from someone close by, and the person they knew who lived the closest and had a surfboard was Cindy. Jules pulled up the station wagon in front of her house and got out like he was facing execution. In the week since the disastrous staying-out-all-night giant-luring party, Cindy's parents had threatened to call the police on Laurie, Jules, and Nick for burglary (of Cindy's father's prized fish) and wanton destruction of property (that part was all Sandspur). It was only their own daughter's involvement in the whole thing that seemed to make them reconsider.

Luckily, there was no car currently in the driveway. Which Nick really hoped meant that Cindy's parents weren't home. Maybe they could just get the surfboard and go.

Mallory got out of the car and stretched, yawning. She seemed to have a bit more color. "This is your girlfriend's house?" she asked Jules.

"Yeah," Jules said quietly.

Nick decided that as the least miserable or sick person out of the station wagon, it was his job to knock on the door. Which he did.

Cindy opened it a few moments later. "You have to get out of here! If my parents see you— look, you just really shouldn't be here."

From behind her, in the house, they heard her father's voice. "Those little sociopaths! What do they want? They come back to murder the rest of my fish?"

"How come you haven't called me?" Jules asked, clearly

completely forgetting the reason they'd come.

"My dad took my cell phone," Cindy whispered. "Right after he grounded me *forever*."

"You could have e-mailed me or something," Jules said. "When I didn't hear from you at all, I didn't know what to think."

"Computer privileges suspended," Cindy said, her hand going to her hip. She looked past him at Mallory, who was leaning against the car, her glossy black hair blowing in the breeze as she checked the ties on her sword. "Who's that?"

Jules looked over. "A friend of my brother's."

"Oh, right! Sure! Your brother is a real..." She wasn't whispering anymore.

"We need to borrow your surfboard," Nick interrupted.

Cindy seemed to deflate. She sighed. "It's

around the side. Take the longboard. Is that the only reason you came over?"

"I've been texting you all week," Jules said.

"Tell them that if they step one foot in this house," her dad yelled from inside, "I am going to use them as chum! Chum, I tell you!"

"Are you sure you can't come with us?" Nick asked. "We could really use the help."

"I really better not," Cindy said before she shut the door.

Jules stared at it a moment, then shook his head and went to get the board.

The beach was windswept, and rough waves crashed against the shore, throwing up enough spray to coat Nick's arms with a fine dusting of salt. Even in the late afternoon there were still surfers out in the swells and a small group of sunbathers spread out on towels. Nick wanted to scream at them. Didn't they know about the sinkholes? Weren't they worried?

"I can't take the nixies out there," Jules said to Nick as they clambered down from the highest dune, where the car was parked, past palm trees and sea grapes to the compacted sand and shell of the beach.

Mallory walked up to Jules without her shoes on. Simon and Jared were behind her. "You ready?"

Jules shook his head. "I can't do this. I can't be the one to go out there."

"What?" Mallory asked him.

"Merfolk took him underwater. For a while," said Nick. He didn't want to say anything else, not about Jules's nightmares or the fact that Jules no longer went to the beach each morning. He wasn't sure they'd understand.

"We can't surf," Jared said. "We live in the *middle of Maine*. We only know how to swim in pools."

Nick saw Jules start to say something and was suddenly afraid that Jules would volunteer to go out on the water when he wasn't ready. Nick started talking before Jules could. "I'll go. I'll take the surfboard and a nixie out into the water."

"You're going to go?" Jules asked, looking at Nick in alarm.

"I'll go," Nick repeated, toeing off his shoes and trying to convince himself that he wasn't terrified. The hot sand scalded the soles of his feet. "I'll go out there with the surfboard and one of the nixies."

After their mother died, their dad had come up with a long list of things that were too dangerous to do, including swimming in the

ocean. Jules got around some of that because he'd already spent all his weekends in the ocean, but Nick hadn't been swimming in ages. He grabbed the board from where Jules had dumped it in the sand.

Mallory glanced toward the wagon, where

the nixies huddled in the backseat in their towels. Laurie was talking to them, keeping them calm. "Do you trust them?"

"Barely," Nick said.

"They'll help one another," Jared said. "Nick brings out one of the nixies on the surfboard. We can have another nixie in the car and maybe a third nixie somewhere else. That way, when one of the nixies stops singing, another one starts."

Nick nodded. "And the singing lures in the giants, and we bring them to a sinkhole. Right."

"There is only one way that I'm letting you do this," Jules said. "You have to promise to get back to the car before we drive away. We're not leaving you on the shore."

Jared started to say something—maybe to object—but he closed his mouth at Jules's glare.

"Okay," Nick said. He didn't want to admit how relieved he felt at the idea that he wouldn't be out in the ocean with a nixie, dodging giants, while everyone else drove away. "How far out in the water do I have to go?"

"We should practice," Jared said. "Swim out a ways and then we'll time how fast you can get in to shore."

Jules pointed. "How about to that sandbar? That seems far enough."

"You can swim, right?" Mallory asked him.

"*Yes*," Nick said, and headed off toward the water.

Paddling out on Cindy's floral-patterned longboard, the scent of pineapple surf wax in his nose, gulping mouthfuls of salty water, Nick concentrated on the fact that whatever happened, at least he was trying. He was really trying. He had always thought that if he really

Overleaf
Previously lost drawings
rendered by Arthur Spiderwick.
Retrieved by Jared Grace
from Noseeum Jack's residence.

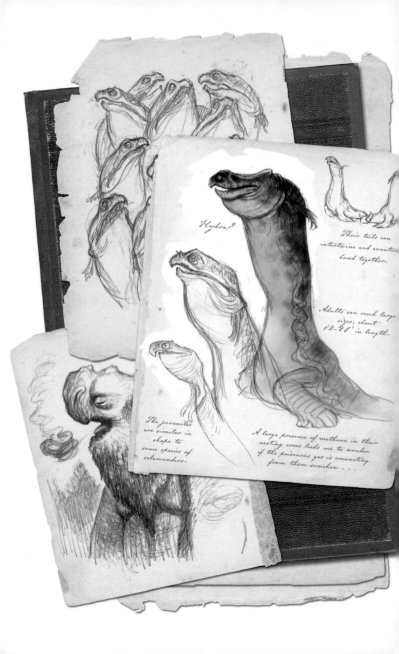

Hydra?

Their tails can intertwine and eventually bond together.

Adults can reach large sizes, about 12-20' in length.

The juveniles are similar in shape to some species of salamanders.

A large presence of methane in their nesting areas leads me to wonder if the poisonous gas is emanating from them somehow . . .

put in an effort and things didn't work out, that would be worse than never trying at all. But, kicking with his back legs and holding his breath as water crashed over his head, he realized that one good thing about this was that if he failed, he probably wouldn't live long enough to feel bad about it.

He looked back at Jules standing on the beach. Laurie was standing beside him. He wasn't quite to the sandbar yet. He guessed he'd better go out farther.

For a moment Nick thought he saw something in the waves. A dark shape. Then the crest of a swell broke over him and he was thrown under the waves.

He spun upside down, and his board crashed down on his head, stunning him. The pain made him gasp, drinking down water. He struggled toward the surface, panicking,

"What do you wish to tell us?"

and felt his hand touch sand. He had been swimming the wrong way.

Lungs burning, he pushed off the ocean floor. Light was above him now, but he didn't have any air left. Everything was going fuzzy and black at the edges.

Then in front of him was a face with hair flowing around it in a nimbus. For a moment she looked like his mother, and then her mouth touched his and his vision cleared. Air—sweet air. He took a breath from her lips and then another.

He looked around and there they were—merfolk. They swam in circles, their long fins seeming to float, their scaly tails lashing the water languorously. A swirling vortex of bodies, circling him in tandem.

"What do you wish to tell us?" they said together. He couldn't have really heard them—the sound

of any voice would be swallowed by the sea—but he could see their mouths move and somehow understood them.

He made a frantic gesture toward his mouth. Now that the mermaid was no longer feeding him air, he couldn't hold his breath much longer.

One of the mermaids swam close and gave him a cap of woven sea grass. She mimed putting it on, so he did.

She opened her mouth and gestured toward it. He shook his head, making a strangling motion. She shook her head, and he finally opened his mouth a little ways. He gasped and a little bubble formed around his mouth. A bubble full of briny air. He could breathe.

"I'm sorry about the giants," he said. The bubble burst, and his voice came from it. A new bubble formed.

"*We do not believe you,*" they said, and there was no mistaking that he heard their voices this time—a strange, deep echo, like whale song. "*You tricked us.*"

"I'm really sorry. And we want to get the giants out of the water now. We're trying to make up for it."

"*We warned you about the balance,*" they said.

"We should have listened. Please just let us lure them out again. It'll be like it never happened."

"*We will not help you, land dweller.*"

"But I thought you didn't want them here in the water."

"*We do not, but now that they are here, they are ours to protect. They are closer kin than you.*"

"There are creatures. Dragons—I don't know, but—"

"*We people of the sea have longer memories than*

those of the land. We know of the hydras forming now. We wished for the land to burn. Now it will."

"Please," Nick said.

"Good-bye, land dweller."

Suddenly Nicholas found himself rising through the waves to sputter at the surface.

Laurie was paddling nearby, her body on top of Cindy's surfboard, calling his name.

"I'm right here," Nick yelled before he choked on another mouthful of water. The cap was still clutched in one hand.

"What is that?" Laurie asked, gesturing toward the cap.

He opened his mouth to answer her, but he gulped sea instead. Then, sputtering, he said, "It's for breathing underwater. From the merfolk."

She reached out her hand. "We should never have let you come out by yourself," she said. "I thought you'd drowned!" She looked angry.

He swam over and held on to the board, panting. Together, they let the current push them back to shore and then staggered up the beach. Nick collapsed on the sand.

"Merfolk," said Nick. "They're glad we're going to be destroyed. I think that's pretty much exactly what they want."

The giants followed the car.

Chapter Six

IN WHICH Everybody Runs

Sitting on the sand as Sandspur dug a hole, they went over and over what the merfolk told Nick. Up at the wagon the nixies looked down accusingly from their towels.

"I think the merfolk thought I was going out there to ask for help," he said. "I don't think they know we have another plan."

Jared looked out at the ocean and tilted his head as he sketched the landscape. "They probably don't think there is any other way of getting out the giants. They may never have even seen a nixie — I mean, they didn't seem to know you could get a fish from far away."

"Still, they're faeries!" Laurie said.

Nick's first urge was to snap at Laurie that it was faeries who'd gotten them into this mess, but he didn't. He could blame faeries, or Laurie, or himself, but it wouldn't help. What they needed now was a way out.

"I think we should go through with the plan," Nick said. "Just the way that we intended."

"The nixies won't agree to that," Laurie said.

"We won't tell them," said Nick, and then, seeing her expression, he frowned. "Oh, come on, like *you're* going to act like you suddenly have an objection to *lying*. Anyway, technically we won't even *be* lying — just not telling the nixies absolutely everything. So they don't worry."

Laurie rolled her eyes but didn't say anything.

Jared looked out at the ocean.

"It's too dangerous," said Jules.

"He's right," said Mallory, with a nod toward Jules.

"Oh yeah," said Jared. "Because you're all about safety, Mallory."

Nick sighed. "Do any of you have a better idea?"

Jared looked at the surfers and the sunbathers. "I don't have a better idea. I think Nick's right. I'll even go with him."

"We should try," said Simon, staring at the sand. "We've tried dumber things."

Mallory whirled on him. "You're on Jared's side?"

Simon held up the jar with the dragons. They had grown so much that one of their heads had dented the top of the jar. "We need to do *something*. Now."

Nick got up. "Look, everything about this

plan is dangerous, but it's my decision how I do my part. And it's Jared's decision if he wants to come with me."

"Dad would kill you for even thinking of going out in the water," Jules said. "And he would kill me for letting you."

Nick didn't want to point out that their dad's killing them required the optimistic assumption that they'd make it home alive. "I know," he said instead, getting up.

"You know, you could be a politician when you grow up, with all your promises and your deals and your technically not lying," Mallory said to Nick as he walked up to convince one of the nixies that everything was going according to plan.

Nick had never really considered a career in politics, but if he pulled this off, he might have to give it some thought.

As Nick and Jared swam against the tide, pushing the surfboard carrying Ibi out into deeper water, Taloa got stationed down the beach with Laurie, while Jules, Simon, Mallory, and Ooki stayed in the wagon with the hatch window down so that Ooki's singing would be more audible.

Above them thunder cracked, and rain began to fall. Ibi seemed to brighten beneath it. She shook out the strange tendrils of her hair and raised her webbed hands to collect drops of it.

"I'd love to draw her," Jared said to Nick.

Nick nodded, but he wasn't really paying attention. Wearing the sea grass cap, he watched the waves for merfolk.

He didn't see anything, but the water seemed to get rougher, the waves larger. They paddled frantically out, cresting a wave just before it broke over them. He could feel a riptide pulling them away from the shore. It was like the whole sea was angry with him.

Ibi hissed as salt water splashed her. Her skin looked pinker and more puckered where it hit.

Nick considered suggesting going back. Maybe ignoring the merfolk's warning had been the result of some kind of bravado mixed with banging his head when he'd gotten tossed around in the surf.

Just then Ibi began to sing. Strands of her song floated through the air.

Jared stared at Ibi as though in a daze. Even the not-so-far-off surfers stopped paddling. Nick wasn't sure what they heard without the Sight; maybe everything. The music washed over him, sweet and pure. He never wanted it to stop.

The distant rocks were changing, unwinding

"Keep singing!"

themselves, pushing to unsteady feet. The rain began to fall harder.

"Keep singing!" Nick yelled. "We have to start toward the beach."

Ibi sang, louder and louder. A wave flung the surfboard forward, and Nick and Jared were left treading water behind it. Nick grabbed hold of the edge and scrabbled to get up on it with Ibi. He reached for Jared.

The giants were coming, their mountainous forms lurching toward Ibi. The waves grew even rougher, each swell threatening to capsize the surfboard.

Then came a huge wave. It crested above them like a shadow.

"Oh, no," said Nick, pulling at Jared's wrist. "You need to get up here before that hits."

Jared was half-kicked and half-pulled onto the board. It tipped to the side and Ibi keened, nearly falling off. She grabbed hold of Nick with moist, rubbery fingers.

The wave frothed and curled as though eager to topple them.

"This is going to be bad, isn't it?" Jared asked.

"Oh yeah," said Nick, and gripped the board as tightly as he could.

Somewhere in the distance the nixies on the shore had taken up the song.

Then the wave crashed down on the surf-board.

Nick held on to the board as it spun underwater. He could feel Ibi's arms around him, and one of Jared's feet kicked him as they were knocked around under the waves. Then he felt the scrape of shells and sand as the wave tossed them all onto the beach.

Nick coughed. He was pretty sure he'd

skinned his knee. Taloa and Laurie started running for the car. Only Ooki still sang.

"Get up!" Jared yelled, yanking Nick to his feet. "They're coming."

Ibi was already hopping toward the station wagon, her slippery rain-drenched movements swifter than he would have guessed possible. Nick didn't look back at the water as Jared sped ahead. Nick just tried to run toward the station wagon as fast as his waterlogged body could go. Ibi was already hopping into the back of the wagon, and Jared threw himself into the backseat. Mallory hauled Nick inside.

Giants crashed onto the beach a moment later.

"Go," Nick said, slamming the door. "Gogogogogo."

Jules hit the gas and they pulled out of the parking lot with a screech. Just like they'd planned, the giants followed the car.

Please, Nick told the universe silently. *Please let no one get in the way of those giants.*

Jules pulled onto the highway. It was mostly deserted, which meant it was probably dotted with sinkholes. The few cars veered off the road as the giants lurched into view, and Nick could only imagine what they saw. A landslide of moving rock.

Jules drove in front of a sinkhole gaping across one lane and off the road. The car screeched to a halt, tearing up the grass and dirt with the tires as it pulled onto the shoulder. Taloa stopped singing and they waited.

The giants crashed toward them as Nick consigned himself to a certain and messy death.

But as they got close, the first giant scented the air, nostrils flaring. It went still. Then it headed for the sinkhole. The others—about a dozen— followed its lead, moving toward the station wagon and the enormous crater in the ground.

"We've got to get out of here," Jules said. He eased his foot down on the gas and they began to drift slowly toward the road.

One of the giants jumped into the pit with a groan. He began to reach down and fill his mouth with sand and wriggling black things. The others reached down too.

"It's working," Mallory said.

Taloa touched the window with the wide pads of her fingertips.

Then, suddenly, one of the giants roared and turned to the other. Fire blew out of its mouth in a great gust, causing the other to throw its arms over its face.

Laurie screamed.

Out of the pit rolled a black hydra, its dragon bodies twisted and tangled together into a single mass. One of the giants grabbed hold of the wriggling mass and, lifting it up, dumped it into its mouth. It turned toward the giant in the pit and exhaled a long line of flames that caught all along the pit itself. The giant within bellowed and clawed at the sides.

"I think we messed up again," Nick yelled. "This can't be the right thing. This can't be good."

"They're eating the dragons," Simon said. "But they're going to set fire to everything."

"We have to do something!"

"What?" Jules said, hitting the gas harder. They

were moving away from the fire and smoke, away from the giants and away from any answers.

Jules pulled the car over to the side of the road. He flipped on the radio. The newscaster said there had been a wave large enough to blot out the sun. Others said that rocks had crashed down from nowhere.

"Ibi is hurt," Taloa sang.

Nick looked back. The nixie's skin looked puffy and raw. She moaned.

"The salt," Nick said.

"Get her into the rain," said Laurie.

The kids scrambled out and helped Ibi to stand. She sighed as rain touched her skin.

Sirens wailed in the distance.

Ooki began to sing softly as Taloa glowered.

"What's that?" Mallory asked. She was pointing out to the water, where four more giants were heading for land. "Give me the keys!"

Jules hesitated a moment and then threw them to her as they all scrambled into the car.

It took longer for the giants to make their way out of the deep this time. When they came from the ocean, they were dripping with strands of sea grass, and when they shook their great bodies, bits of coral flew off them.

Mallory turned the wheel hard and pulled onto the road, driving like a lunatic. In this particular instance, Nick could only be glad.

Simon closed his eyes. "I can't look," he said.

"Sing," Nick called to Taloa.

"*No la-lo,*" she sang softly. "*Why should we not la-lo-la be la safe? We do la not want them to fa-la-lo follow.*"

"We can bring them to another sinkhole," he said. "Please."

"Please," said Laurie.

This is the last la-lo-le time, Lauranathana, Taloa sang. *Ibi was hurt. There is nothing more la-lo to offer la-lee us, and in the rain, we can go la-lo anywhere we like.*

"I know," Nick said.

In the back Taloa's song swelled impossibly loud. The earth shook as the giants began to follow them.

The car careered down an unfamiliar street, giants lumbering after it.

"Jules, I think I made a wrong turn," Mallory said.

Jules fumbled with the glove compartment. He pulled out a map, but he couldn't seem to get it to unfold.

"You live here," she yelled. "Don't you know where we are?"

"I don't go this way," Jules shouted back, looking frantically at the map. "Turn here!"

She did, making a turn so sharp that the nixie's song turned into a shriek. A black pit gaped before them like a yawning mouth. They hit the sinkhole before the screeching brakes could have any effect. The car tipped in headfirst.

Nick was thrown forward against the seat in front of him. The jar of dragons flew out of the backseat to crack against the dashboard. The front end of the car folded like paper as it struck the ground.

For a moment everything was silent.

"Is everyone okay?" Mallory shouted, frantic.

"La-lo-le," sang Ibi, *"the air is strange."*

Nick tried to push open the door, first with his hands and then by kicking it. "We're stuck," he said.

"My car!" Jules said. "My poor car."

Mallory hit the button for the windows, but nothing happened.

"Forget about the car. We have to get out," said Nick. The air *was* strange. He gasped but couldn't seem to fill his lungs. Nick saw flames start to lick up along the hood.

"Uh," Simon called. "The methane!"

Mallory reacted faster than the rest of them. Sucking in her breath, she crawled back past the nixies to kick the back window of the station wagon, again and again, until the glass cracked and began to splinter. Until she busted it open.

Mallory climbed through and then reached down for them. "Quick," she said.

Through the windshield Nick saw the dragons. A single seething tangle, they were no longer particularly small. A moving carpet. He felt light-headed.

"Go!"

"Quick, Jared! Simon! Come on!" Mallory said again.

They clambered out, Jules pushing their feet so that Mallory could pull them through. Ooki. Taloa. Ibi. Sandspur. Simon. Laurie. Jared.

Nick wriggled up so that Mallory had to half-haul him through the back window. Behind him, the fire leaped.

"Go!" she said. "I'll get your brother."

As Mallory leaned down for Jules, Nick looked up and saw a giant looming over them. Its face looked as hard as a cliff, its eyes as black as blobs of ink. Its hand reached out for him.

Nick screamed as he was swept up into the air.

He looked back to see Mallory and Jules staring openmouthed after him. Then he was in front of a massive mouth filled with sand, shells, and muddy, cracked teeth.

The grip the creature had on him slackened for a second as it prepared to drop Nick into its gaping maw. Yelling, Nick jumped for the giant's head. His fingers scrabbled at the rock-hard skin, and he slid until he managed to grab hold of an ear.

The giant reached back for him. Nick screamed in terror, right into the giant's ear.

The giant bellowed in pain.

Nick wedged his foot into the giant's ear as it dipped forward and shook its head like a dog trying to shake off water. He had never been so terrified.

Then, catching sight of something on the ground, the giant stilled. Mallory stood in the middle of the road, holding up her sword. It looked as tiny as a toothpick.

The giant ran toward her as Nick held on tight, tighter than he'd held the surfboard.

Nick screamed as he was swept up.

Tighter than he'd held on to anything in his life.

The giant reached out toward Mallory and she lunged. Her sword went through its palm. The giant made a low sound and pulled up its hand. The sword gleamed in the light, buried nearly to the hilt on one side of the giant's hand, the tip sticking out the other side.

Mallory looked up at Nick. She was totally unarmed.

The giant's other hand swung at Mallory. This time it wasn't grabbing, though. This time it was a fist coming to squash her into the asphalt.

A dark-skinned man pushed her out of the way. His long coat swirled around his ankles as he swung an enormous sword at the giant. It cut the giant at the wrist, causing it to stumble back.

Nick looked around frantically. The street

was deserted. Where had the man come from?

"Hold on!" the man yelled up to Nick. Out of his coat he pulled a folded grappling hook attached to a long rope. He swung it around three times, the hook arcing over the man's head before he hurled it toward the giant. One of the prongs sank into the creature's skin. Even as the giant roared and swatted at him, the man started to climb.

Mallory got up from where she'd been tossed and grabbed hold of the rope. She inched her way up it, even as the giant flailed.

Nick climbed out of the curves of the giant's ear, lowering himself toward the puckered flesh and the hook.

"Stay where you are!" the man yelled.

"Get off the rope," Nick shouted back. "I'm coming down."

The giant's hand scraped over its chest, where

the grappling hook was lodged. It didn't come loose, but Mallory and the man swung wildly. Mallory shrieked and let go, falling backward into the dirt below.

Nick held on to the giant's shoulder and then, taking a deep breath and closing his eyes, let himself slip toward the rope. He fell faster and faster, and no amount of grabbing on to the rocky skin was slowing his descent. Grasping for the hook, he felt the hot metal and then the sudden snap of his weight, pulling him away from it. One hand slipped free, and his other hand was sliding off the hook.

Then he felt an arm close around his waist.

"I've got you," the man said. This close, he looked familiar.

The giant swept its arm up, like it was going to try to knock away the hook, but just then an explosion rocked the ground. The giant turned.

His other hand was sliding off the hook.

A ball of flame rose from the sinkhole, followed by the black smoke of Jules's still-burning car.

Nick let go of the hook and closed his eyes, praying the man wouldn't let him fall. Nick scrambled to swing his leg around the rope and hold on to it.

"Lock your arm," the man said, and Nick tried to, closing his arm around the rope and holding his elbow with his other hand. He gritted his teeth.

"We're going down and we have to be fast," yelled the man.

The giant pawed at his chest.

Nick climbed downward as fast as he could, the swinging rope burning his hand. When he got close enough, he jumped and rolled. Then Jules and Laurie and Mallory were there, pulling him to his feet. Jared and Simon raced over with the nixies and Sandspur.

Fire engines wailed as they all ran toward a nearby food stand, its windows boarded up but a radio still on. It seemed like someone had left in a hurry.

"You're Jack's son," Nick said, suddenly placing the man who'd saved him. Jack's son looked very different without his fancy suit. He looked different holding a sword.

The man nodded. "Jack Junior at your service. I couldn't let you handle this on your own. Besides," he said with a grin, "I've been training for this my whole life."

"Hey." Nick tried to catch his breath. "You said giants didn't exist!"

Jack Jr. leaned on his sword. "Okay, would you believe I thought maybe you'd need a lawyer?"

It was he who had forgotten.

Chapter Seven

IN WHICH Nick Fulfills His Promises

U nder the eaves of the little grocery, with the radio playing, they considered what supplies they had left. The car map Jules had stuck in his pocket. Jack Jr.'s sword and a machete he had strapped to his hip under the coat. A cell phone. One woven sea grass cap from the merfolk. Not much. Jack Jr. and Mallory were comparing notes on what they could possibly scavenge from a hardware store to stand in for an extra broadsword when Taloa hopped up to Nick. She smelled like sea grass and mud as she wound her hands around his neck.

"La-le-lo it is time to take us to our stream. The stream you promised la-lee."

"We can't go now," Laurie said, pointing toward the sinkhole and the giants.

"He promised his life la-lo-lee," Taloa sang.

"But you didn't mean . . ." Laurie didn't finish the sentence. Sandspur clawed at her leg and she lifted him up.

Just then Jules's phone rang and he touched his pocket. "That's got to be Dad."

"Don't answer it," Nick said.

"Give me the phone," said Laurie, dropping Sandspur again. He squealed in protest.

"Hello?" she said. "Yes, it's me, Laurie. No, we're fine, but all the roads are blocked off. We've been in traffic for forever. No, we had the radio on. We didn't hear the phone ringing."

Nick grinned at her and she grinned back, as

though she'd forgotten to be angry.

"Yes," she said into the phone, "I'll tell them. I'm really glad they're here with me. I was so scared."

Nick rolled his eyes and Laurie grinned wider.

"I'll see you and Mom when we get there," she said, and hung up.

"Wow," said Jared, shaking his head in admiration. "You're good."

Jules looked up at the storm-bright sky. "I'm starving. It's got to be dinnertime, even if you can barely tell in this weather."

"Yeah," said Jared. "I could even eat one of those dragons if someone put enough mustard on it."

"*La-lo-le Nicholas,*" sang Taloa, winding her arms more tightly around Nick, making his skin crawl. He wished he could push her away, but her arms felt as solid as wood.

"On your life you promised."

"Look," said Nick. "Where's the nearest body of freshwater we can think of?"

"Well, it's not much, but there's a stream that runs behind Cindy's house," Jules said. "It opens into a bigger stream. They'd just have to follow it."

Taloa sighed, air whistling through her nose.

"We'll take you and your sisters," said Nick. "See? I promised, and I'm going to do it."

Taloa's golden eyes were so close to his own that looking into them made him dizzy. *"You promised any body of water we chose la-lo."*

Dread gnawed at Nick's stomach. "But it's a good stream," he said desperately.

"On your life you promised lo-le," sang Taloa.

Laurie put her hand on the nixie's shoulder. "Please, Taloa. I know you're mad that Ibi got hurt, but we all got hurt."

Taloa stepped closer to her sisters. *"La-le so long as it is a very good stream."*

"We can walk to Cindy's from here," said Jules.

"We need to arm ourselves," said Jack Jr. "We need to go back and put an end to the giants as soon as possible."

Nick looked over at Jules.

"Uh," said Jules.

"We're not trying to defeat giants," said Nick.

Jack Jr. looked dazed. "I don't understand."

"We need the giants to eat hydras." Nick felt awkward telling him, since they all had thought the giants were the big threat, the only threat. It was humbling how much there was still to know about a fantastical world with the power to destroy theirs. "If the giants don't eat the dragons, the dragons could grow until they're unstoppable. Dragons will breed out of control, form into hydras, and breathe methane to knock out their prey, and that will be that."

"We can't leave giants roaming around town," said Jack Jr. "Even if they do some good, they're going to do more harm. They're going to step on buildings and knock over cars. People are going to die."

A gust of wind made the rain hit Nick's face like a slap.

"La-lo-la, you said we would go," sang Taloa. Ibi and Ooki huddled close to her.

"Do not break your promise," sang Ibi.

"Do not break your promise," sang Ooki.

"It's our job to not let people die," Jack Jr. said.

Their job? Nick thought of a million ways that wasn't true, a million excuses, but all he said was, "I know."

Simon cleared his throat. "What if those sinkholes aren't really separate? I've been thinking about the pattern that we saw on television and also about the high concentration of giants in this particular area and—"

"You're saying you think that all the sink-holes are connected," said Nick. "One massive sinkhole opening up underneath us? But that would mean that there's a ton of displaced soil. Too much, I think."

"Wow," said Mallory. "You two realize that no one else understands what you're saying, right? But it's great you've found each other."

"The soil underneath is being eroded, probably by pockets of eggs hatching, creating gaps," Simon said. "Maybe the sinkholes don't actually connect aboveground, but I bet they're connected belowground."

Jared shook his head. "Eggs? Wait a minute, if there are eggs, then I'm not sure I want to see what's laying them."

Nick nodded. "After reading the pages, we

thought something was waking up, but you're right—these things look like they're just being born. Jules, give me the map." He looked at Taloa. "This will help us get to the stream, too, I swear."

"Many promises la-lo," she sang.

Nick unfolded the map on the damp cement under the flickering grocery light. Simon leaned over his shoulder. Nick tried to remember the television screen and the positions of the sinkholes.

"Does anyone have pins?"

No one did, but Nick found some change and dropped a penny on each part of the map where he knew there was a sinkhole.

"Where are the rest of them?" he asked the huddled group.

"We could change the channel on the radio," Jules said, pointing up at the speaker.

"I think I could pry off one of these boards," Mallory said.

A few minutes later they'd flipped the channel to a weather report.

"Winds are high, blowing down trees. Small localized twisters reported. Advisory notice to stay inside."

"Think people will stay inside?" Nick asked.

"That will only help some," said Jack Jr. "It's safer there, but not by much."

"Three more sinkholes opened. Avoid Route 10 at the intersection of—"

Nick dropped pennies onto the map as each address was called out. The copper pieces gleamed in the reflection of the grocery store's lights.

"What are you doing that for?" Mallory asked, leaning over him.

"Look," Nick said. He set a quarter down in the center of the sinkholes they'd pinpointed. "All

"Look."

we've seen in the sinkholes are baby dragons. I bet whatever is hatching these things is right there."

Jules squinted. "That's behind the old mall."

Simon and Jared exchanged a glance. "One dragon is enough—if it's a full-size hydra *made* of dragons, we're in real trouble."

"Okay," Jack Jr. said. "If you're going to take the nixies, you better get going." He touched the map. "We'll check out the nearest sinkhole. I'm ready to chop up some hydras if need be."

Jules nodded. "Laurie and I should go with Nick. Then we'll find you."

"Keep your phone on," Mallory said.

With a look back at Jack Jr. and the three Grace kids, Nick set off with his brother and stepsister to try to lead the three nixies to the nearest, safest stream he knew of. The nixies sang together softly, a little song that made Nick smile.

"Are you scared?" Laurie asked, shifting

Sandspur's weight to her other hip.

Nick nodded. "You?"

"I don't know if we're doing the right thing anymore. It all seems so complicated."

"Wet," said Sandspur. "I hate the wet. Cold and wet." He shook his head like he could shake himself dry in the downpour. "And hungry."

Nick laughed—seeing something more miserable than he was cheered him, even though he knew the feeling was uncharitable. "I'm glad I get a chance to tell you that I'm sorry about what happened with your mom and my dad."

Laurie clutched Sandspur closer and looked down. "I know it's not your fault. I know that, even if I don't act like it."

"I could have seemed happier about stuff."

"Do you want us not to live together?"

Nick shrugged.

"You don't, do you?"

"I didn't," said Nick. "It's not like I didn't like you. Or Charlene. It's just that it all happened so fast. All of a sudden you were — I don't know — invading my territory."

"Well, now we're out of your way."

"Oh, come on, our house is gone. I was dumb. I'm glad you're my sister."

Laurie smiled at him. "Stepsister," she said.

They walked through the wet brush, down empty streets, and cut through the backyards of houses. It didn't seem so far to walk now that Laurie wasn't mad at him.

"Hey," called Jules. "We found it."

The nixies were already sliding into the stream when Nick and Laurie walked up. Taloa raised a webbed hand.

"La-lo-le we will not meet again."

"But—," Laurie started.

"Good-bye," Nick said.

"We'll miss you," Laurie put in.

The nixies sank under the dark surface, raindrops making the ripples hard to see. Nick wasn't sure if he could pick out their shapes as they moved under the water.

Laurie stared at the water with a kind of fierce longing.

"Come on," Nick said, putting a hand on her shoulder, gently turning her around so they could begin stumbling back toward the sinkholes.

They followed Jules through several backyards. Nick said, "Aren't we supposed to be going that way?" He pointed in a direction slightly to the left of where they were headed.

Jules shrugged uncomfortably. "I thought we could cut through Cindy's lawn."

"Is that really a shortcut?" Nick asked, looking around. It seemed to him that Cindy's house was in the wrong direction. "Plus her dad wouldn't be thrilled to see us."

"It's close by," Jules said. "I just want to know she's all right."

"We have to be quick," Laurie said.

"I know," Jules said, and then, seeing the expression on Nick's face, looked away. "We'll be quick," he said.

They shuffled through bushes, pushing aside honeysuckle vines, and stepped into Cindy's backyard. They could see clearly a split in the earth near one of the trees, as though a sinkhole was forming.

They stopped.

"That tree is going to fall right on the house," Jules said, his voice sounding hollow from horror.

"Ring the doorbell—tell them," Nick said. "But then we really have to go. We have to go, Jules."

Laurie yelled from behind them, a shout that was smothered. Nick looked back in time to see her slide deeper into the ground. Somehow the gap had widened, and now he could see only the top of Laurie's head as she disappeared into the crack in the earth. Sandspur danced on her head, pulling at her hair, until he stepped wrong and slipped down beside her.

"Laurie!" Jules shouted, throwing himself

SANDSPUR

on his stomach and crawling toward her. He reached out a hand into the muddy crevice, digging around to get hold of her. Nick, stunned, rushed to help just as the earth split in a wide seam, creating a hole.

Laurie caught Jules's hand. Spitting dirt and struggling like she wasn't sure where she was, she dangled over the new pit. Sandspur fell to the bottom and headed for the side, where he scratched at the dirt wall.

"Hold on, Laurie!" Nick shouted. He pounded on Cindy's door and shouted, "We need help! Help!"

The door opened and Cindy stuck her head out. "Oh, that's bad," she said.

Her father raced out after Cindy.

"Cindy, come back inside," her mother called.

"Get a rope or something," Nick said, and threw himself down on his knees next to Jules, trying to reach for Laurie's other hand.

"The tree!" Cindy yelled.

Jules looked up, and all the color seemed to drain out of his face. He didn't speak, he just let go of Laurie and lunged at Nick. Nick fell on his back, away from the seam in the earth.

Laurie screamed.

With a *crack* the tree fell where Jules had been standing. Nick felt the whoosh of it without fully comprehending, and a few thin branches scraped his cheek. Then everything seemed to go quiet.

"Jules?" he said.

Laurie seemed to be sobbing in the pit where Jules had dropped her.

Somehow, Cindy and her father were already pushing the tree. "Nick!" she yelled. "We need your help."

In a daze Nick fought through the branches to get to where Jules was. His face looked pale in the moonlight, and his eyes were closed. Part of the trunk was holding down his legs.

"Help us move it!" Cindy's dad shouted.

Nick threw his weight against the tree, groaning. Cindy and her dad heaved at the same time, and the trunk rolled in the mud, away from the pit and off of Jules.

Jules's eyes fluttered open. "Nick?"

"I'm okay," Nick said. "You got me out of the way."

"I can't feel my leg," Jules said, and shut his eyes again.

"Do something," Nick said to Cindy. "We have to get him inside!"

Cindy's dad shook his head and took off his raincoat, spreading it over Jules's body. "We shouldn't. You're not supposed to move someone who's been in an accident until you know what kind of injuries they've sustained."

"What do we do?" Cindy touched Jules's hair. "We can't just leave him in the rain."

"Okay, we can try and carry him into the house," Cindy's dad said. "But we're going to have to be careful and move slowly."

"Go get your sister out of that pit," said Cindy to Nick. "We can manage here."

Nick nodded, trying to take deep breaths and not panic. He wanted to shake Jules hard enough to wake him, but he knew he had to force himself to walk over to the edge of the sinkhole.

Laurie was huddled against one side at the bottom, a few tiny bodies snaking around her. She looked like the methane was making her woozy, but she was still awake and breathing. In the center of the sinkhole was a creature the size of a dog, large-bellied and growing as it stuffed handfuls of black dragonets into its mouth. Although its features were distorted and strange, there was something so familiar about it that Nick took a second look. At its feet rested the remains of a small broken collar.

The creature was Sandspur. And he was still swelling larger.

"What's happening?" Nick called down.

"Sandspur's not a hobgoblin," she said in a small, unsteady voice. "I don't know what he is—but as the dragon things come up, he keeps eating them before they can turn into hydras."

Maybe that's why there isn't enough methane to make Laurie pass out, Nick thought.

"Hungry," said Sandspur, fixing his gaze on Nick. "You three said you would feed me. You three said you would feed me anything I wanted."

"Uh," said Nick, "okay. Aren't those dragons delicious?"

Sandspur kicked the wall of the sinkhole, and the edge crumbled, sending Nick sliding down on an avalanche of dirt and mud.

"Hey!" Nick said, finding himself trapped in the pit too.

"Still hungry," said the creature, his mouth gaping wider and his weird eyes bulging.

"There's more of them," Nick said, pointing to the dragons, but the few he saw were worming their way back into the dirt to get away from the thing in front of him.

"We'll get you food," said Laurie, moving away from the wall. "We're going to keep his promise."

"Yessss," said Sandspur. "Nick keeps it right now." With that, Sandspur's mouth stretched open wider than Nick could have imagined. Huge jaws closed over him.

He tried to shout, but he was smothered by wet skin. A row of jagged teeth scraped his arm,

"There's more of them."

and then he was sinking into hot, foul-smelling darkness. He was inside Sandspur.

"Auggggh!" he shouted, curled in a ball, beating his hands against the sticky walls of the monster's stomach. A belch shook him.

Outside he could hear Laurie yelling, as from very far away. "Sandspur! What did you do? Did you chew him? You better throw him back up right now."

"He is keeping me full," said Sandspur. The squeaky voice seemed to echo all around Nick.

"I thought you were our friend," Laurie said.

Nick had told her it wasn't safe to trust faeries. He'd told her and told her and told her, but in the end it was he who'd forgotten. He was the one who let them make a rash, dumb promise. And now he'd been eaten up for it.

"Spit him out. Spit him out and I'll give you something else. Something tastier," Laurie said.

"What will you give me?" asked Sandspur.

Quick, Nick thought. *Quick.* With each breath he felt dizzier. The heat and the smell were overwhelming. Things shifted underneath him, and he recalled all the dragons that Sandspur had swallowed. His skin crawled, but he couldn't get away from their wriggling bodies or the methane they were doubtless breathing all around him.

"Cake," Laurie said. Nick could hear her voice breaking. "But you have to help me out."

He felt the creature shift and lurch. Taking another stinking breath, he choked. He couldn't get enough air, and the walls were closing in on him.

"Where do you go?" Nick heard Sandspur say.

"To get the cake," she said. It seemed to him like she was retreating farther into the distance, but perhaps he was passing out. He wasn't thinking clearly. He couldn't keep his eyes open.

"Good," Laurie was saying. "Now just open your mouth and I'll throw it in."

Something hard tumbled down on top of Nick. It struck him on the arm heavily. It felt like a rock.

"That's right—keep your mouth open."

More rocks rained down on Nick, scraping his skin and hitting the side of his head hard enough to draw blood. He flung his arms over his head and only bit back a shout by remembering that if he shouted, he'd be breathing more methane.

Then around him Sandspur shifted. "I can't move! What did you do?"

"I filled you up," Laurie said. "With rocks."

Everything shifted again. "No fair! No fair!"

"Now you better puke, Sandspur. You better throw up right now or you're going to be stuck where you are forever."

"You tricked me!" he howled. "No fair tricking!"

"That's right," said Laurie. "No fair tricking."

Another lurch, and then Nick was thrown forward, out of the stinking darkness onto mud.

Slimy things rained down on him and more rocks struck him, but he sucked in breath after sweet breath of air, and that took all his concentration.

"Nick?" Laurie said from above him. "Are you okay?" She had climbed up into the branches of the toppled tree and was reaching down like she actually wanted him to stand up.

"No," he said, spitting out dirt and slime. "Not okay. Definitely not okay." He was sticky with whatever stuff coated the insides of Sandspur's

stomach, and trying to wipe it off only seemed to spread the goo around.

He turned on his side to see that Sandspur had shrunk down to his old size and was nibbling at the regurgitated dragonets that were wriggling into the walls.

"What just happened?" Nick asked.

"Well, the way he swelled up," she called down, "I think he's a spriggan. But he's probably too sore to do it again for a while."

She kept talking, saying something about an old story about a creature that could inflate itself, but Nick found himself distracted by the bruise on his head and thoughts of Jules. Lightning cracked above them, and in that moment of brightness he saw the walls of the sinkhole where the dragonets had crawled through. They were laced with holes, some slender, others wide. Tunnels.

Made of melted plastic

Chapter Eight

IN WHICH Everything
Begins to Come Apart

The way back to Jack Jr. and the Grace kids was soggy and miserable. Nick still felt light-headed from the methane, and his skin itched from being inside Sandspur. The rain should have washed the gunk off, but it seemed water resistant. But worst of all, he was left with the memory of Jules lying in the mud, telling them they'd have to go without him.

Nick thought that maybe he should have stayed at Cindy's with his brother. Maybe they should have waited for their dad or an ambulance.

Maybe they'd lured enough giants back in enough time that the giants would eat all the dragonets before they became hydras, before they grew too large to contend with.

But he wanted to make sure.

Laurie walked beside him, and Sandspur trailed after them along the deserted streets. They passed by telephone poles knocked over like dominoes, flickering streetlights, and a Corvette that appeared to have been stepped on.

"You're really okay?" Laurie asked for what must have been the millionth time.

"*Yes,*" Nick said. "Except that he's *following* us. Sandspur, shoo!" Nick waved his hands at the faerie, who then slunk off into the bushes.

"I'm sorry about the rocks," Laurie said to Nick, looking sadly after the little creature.

"Good," he replied, touching a bruise on his temple. "You better be."

She gave him a wan smile. They headed for the sinkhole Jack Jr. had said they'd all be investigating, but Nick was surprised to find them along the road heading back.

"What took you so long?" Mallory asked. "We saw the one sinkhole—there were already two giants digging it up. Our plan was to head for another sinkhole two blocks over in that direction." She nodded her head in the direction they'd been going. "I called Jules, but he didn't answer. Where is he? What happened?"

"He got hurt," Nick said.

"Bad?" Jack Jr. asked.

"I don't know," said Nick.

"He's tough," Mallory said. "He's going to be okay."

Laurie turned to Jared. "How come you didn't tell me Sandspur was a spriggan?" she demanded. "He ate Nick."

"Seriously?" Simon asked.

Jared's eyes went wide. "How was I supposed to know? What's a spriggan?"

"They swell up," Laurie said. "Don't you read any books other than the field guide?"

"Uh, comics?" Jared said.

"Okay, you two, enough," Jack Jr. said, and waited for their silence. "My motorcycle's

not far, but it can only carry me. The nearest sinkholes didn't tell us much except that the giants seem to be eating the dragons at a pretty fast rate. I'm going to go see about behind the old mall. If there is a hydra there—one big enough to be spawning all the dragons—then I should find out."

"I found something," Nick said. "There were holes in the sides of a sinkhole that opened up by Cindy's house. They seemed big enough for the sinkholes to be connected by a network of tunnels."

"That makes it even more important that I go."

"I'll come too," Mallory said.

Jack Jr. shook his head. "You're all really brave, but you're kids."

Nick couldn't help wondering what it was about the Sight that changed you forever. Here was this guy, a successful lawyer, who didn't have to put himself in danger. And yet he was walking toward trouble like there was nowhere in the world he would rather be and nothing he would rather be doing.

Nick wondered how much he'd already been changed by the Sight and how many changes were ones he hadn't even noticed yet.

"I'm not a kid," Mallory said. "I can fight."

Jack Jr. sighed. "I was trained, just like my father was trained before me, to fight giants. Even though I was told that it was going to happen in my lifetime, I didn't want to face it." He took off the leather glove on his left hand, and Nick could see the uneven patches of skin where he'd been burned.

Mallory sucked in her breath.

"All the way up my arm," said Jack Jr., unbuttoning his collar to show more mottled skin. The burns made him look like he was made of melted plastic. He turned to Mallory. "All the way across my chest. It happened when I wasn't all that much older than you. We went out to find a giant that was supposed to be sleeping, but he was up and moving around. A small one—maybe that's why he woke up. And he had a wriggling black worm hanging out of his mouth.

"Dad might have said something to me. I don't really remember. I was terrified, and the only thing I could think to do was attack. I just remember running toward the giant. It nearly killed me."

"Is that when you stopped fighting giants?" Nick asked.

Jack Jr. shook his head. "Not then, but not long after, either. It's hard to fight nature," he said. "If there's something at the center of these sinkholes, then I need to face it for my father."

He reached under his long coat and came out with another blade—a machete. He handed that to Mallory. "In case any giants come your way. It's heavier than you're used to, and you're not going to be able to do those fancy moves you can with a foil."

"Watch me," Mallory said with a grin.

Nick thought Jack Jr. would be offended, but he only grinned back at her. "Wish I could." Then he headed through the rain in the direction of his bike.

For a moment they stood silently on the sidewalk, watching him go.

"Okay." Mallory nodded slowly and shoved the machete into her belt. "Let's get moving."

"Where?" asked Laurie.

"That abandoned mall, where do you think?" said Mallory. "Just because Jack Junior is an adult doesn't mean that we're going to do what he says."

Simon groaned. "Are you serious? We're *on foot.*"

"It's probably a mile-long walk," Mallory said. "Maybe a little more. We can't get there before Jack Junior does, but we'll get there. And if he gets in trouble with whatever he finds at the center of the network of tunnels, he'll be glad to see us."

Nick thought about Jules waking up without any of his family. He thought about their dad not knowing where his kids were. And Laurie—when she first figured out that faeries were real, that the Spiderwick stories were real, this couldn't be how she'd hoped things would end.

"Maybe Jack Junior's right," Nick said. "Maybe we can't really help much at this point. What are we going to do against giants and full-grown hydras?"

Laurie looked at him in surprise. "But you're the one who figured out that there might be an adult hydra. You're the one who found the tunnels in the sinkholes."

"Leave Nick alone," Jared said. "He nearly died."

She frowned at Jared. "I know that. I didn't mean—"

"I've been thinking the same thing," Jared said. "I didn't know the hobgoblin was really a spriggan. Uncle Arthur lost everything trying to beat faeries. And he put everyone he cared about in total danger. I don't want to be like him, but I feel like I am a lot like him. Like I'm making all the same mistakes."

Mallory looked over at him and bit her lower lip. "Is that what's been bothering you?"

Jared nodded.

"Arthur did what he did alone," Mallory said. "We've got each other. And if we do this, it should be because we all agree to do it."

Nick nodded. His head hurt and he was tired and rain-soaked, but at least he could see if Jack Jr. was all right. "Okay."

"Okay," Jared said.

"*Okay,*" said Laurie.

"Yeah, me too," said Simon.

Just then a giant came into view. It took two massive steps and crouched, sniffing the air. Then it sank its fists into the ground. It shredded roots and dirt and pavement to create a hole, stonelike fingers groping in the dirt for a few more wriggling dragonets. Then it walked a few more steps and plunged its hand into the earth again.

"What is it doing?" Mallory asked.

"I think the giants have figured out about the tunnels," said Nick. "I think they're following the dragons back to whatever's at the center of them."

"Look at that!" Simon pointed to where another giant had stepped over a convenience store and was beginning to pull up a tree behind it. Then it started scooping black dragonets into its mouth.

"Headed the same way," said Jared. "Right into Jack Junior's path."

"Nick, you've got to be right. The giants are converging on something." Mallory started running. "Come on!"

They ran through the rain until Nick felt like he was underwater again. Their shoes squelched with each step. Nick's clothes hung on him like weights. He selfishly wished that Jules could have been with them. It's easier being brave with your older brother by your side, being braver.

Eventually, as they passed dark, desolate streets, Nick slowed to a jog. Laurie looked over at him and smiled. She seemed tired, but it was enough to make him pick up his pace.

The old, abandoned mall squatted in the center of a vast parking lot. A newer mall with a better food court and fancier everything had been built about five years ago, closer to the highway. This one closed for renovations soon after.

Now, in the rain and dark, as they crossed the lot and headed for the treeline on the other side, the empty building seemed to flicker with ominous light.

They passed it and saw, to their horror, that

the back half was collapsed and burning, even in the heavy rain. The bodies of two giants draped across the remains. Their skin slowly crumbled into stone.

"This is bad," Simon said.

"Do you want to turn back?" Mallory asked.

"No," said Simon softly. "I'm just pointing out the obvious."

No one else spoke as they entered the mangrove forest behind the mall. Their shoes sank into the thick mud.

It was the noise that first made Nick think something might be close by. There was a booming sound, like thunder. Then the whole world lit up with fire.

In the new light Nick saw three giants, staggering backward, pursued by something that should have been impossible.

Enormous dragons were caught together in a single hydra. Dozens of heads wove hypnotically as it moved in a sickening roll toward the semicircle of six giants surrounding it. A giant approached, trying to grab one of the hydra's heads, but more heads darted and tore at the giant's flesh. It fell back moaning.

The monster converged on the giant so that more and more dragon maws rent the giant's stony flesh until the giant disintegrated into the mud right before their eyes. The giant was dead.

Laurie and Nick ran in the other direction as Simon stared openmouthed.

"Hydra," Simon said softly. "Wyrm king."

The creature seemed to hear him, several pointed heads fixing their pale gaze on him. It slithered forward and the air turned heavy.

"Simon!" Nick yelled, moving backward as fast as he could. Laurie was beside him.

The hydra breathed in the direction of the Grace kids, its many mouths opening and closing. Jared pulled at Simon's arm, like he was urging him to run before they both sagged and fell. Mallory pulled out the machete and threw it toward where Nick and Laurie stood.

It landed in front of Nick, point sticking in the earth and handle in the air, at the same moment Mallory dropped to the ground and went still.

Nick grabbed the machete.

Chapter Nine

IN WHICH Nick Finally Decides What He Wants

Nick grabbed the machete as the giants shuffled back from the enormous hydra. The hydra roiled and seethed, moving across the earth on its hundreds of tiny legs, dozens of maws opening to show thousands of glittering teeth. Terrible black eyes opened and closed, as though deciding which prey to devour first. Lightning flashed overhead and lit those eyes with a glowing greenish light.

This monster had lived for longer than he could imagine, slumbering under the earth, waiting for some instinct to awaken it so it could slake its appetite with everything it came across.

Jared and Mallory and Simon lay unconscious in the dirt, far too close to the hydra. Nick spotted Jack Jr. across the clearing, cradling his leg and slumped against a tree, his face shadowed. His motorcycle was lying on its side, one of the tires as empty as a popped balloon. Nick wasn't sure if Jack Jr. was awake or not.

"Can we drag them?" Laurie asked. "They're going to get stepped on."

"*We're* going to get stepped on."

As Nick took a step

toward the limp bodies of the Grace kids, he saw Jack Jr. shift his weight and start to stand. The man looked over at them, and his mouth opened in surprise and horror.

"Nick! Laurie!" Jack Jr. shouted, waving his arms. "Get out of here." He pushed himself to his feet, and Nick could see there was something wrong with his leg. He limped toward the Grace children. "I'll protect them. You go!"

One by one, Jack Jr. dragged Jared, Simon, and Mallory beneath the tree. Nick could hear one of them cough as they got out of direct exposure to the methane, but they stayed prone. Jack Jr. knelt beside them, sword out to guard them against the giants looming nearby.

"Run!" Jack Jr. called to Nick.

Nick wondered if his dad and Charlene and Jules would have enough time to get out of the area before this thing and its offspring razed the earth. He looked over at Laurie, but she was staring at the hydra as though hypnotized.

"I'm sorry," he told her. That seemed to sum him up pretty well. Sorry.

"We have to do something," Laurie said.

But there was nothing to do. Despite all of Jack's lessons, neither one of them was a warrior like Mallory. And even Mallory hadn't lasted more than a minute. Laurie couldn't even keep her sneakers tied. The laces flopped in the mud as she stepped toward him and put her hand on his arm. And he—he was the most pathetic of all. He couldn't do anything but make models and come up with stupid ideas.

He closed his eyes.

"Nick!" said Laurie. "We really have to do something."

That's what they'd thought. They'd figured that Jack Jr. could use their help and that they'd be able to do something. But Jack Jr. had been right. They were just kids.

Nick opened his eyes again and found himself looking at Laurie's untied shoes. And he had another stupid idea—so stupid that he couldn't help smiling, because it might work.

"How long can you hold your breath?" Nick asked.

"I don't know," she said.

"We have to untangle the knot." He held up the machete. "Chop them apart. They've been like that a long time—they won't even know what to do without one another."

"How can we do that?" she asked.

"We have to get in the middle of them *somehow*."

"Wait," she said. "You want us to *run into the hydra*?"

"No," he said impatiently. "Look, wherever

there have been sinkholes, there have been these tunnels. The dragons tunneled up from wherever they were, tunneled out into the sinkholes. We can crawl through the tunnels too."

"How are we going to breathe?"

"I don't know," Nick said. "There are only two things we have going for us: We're small and have thumbs."

"Nick!"

"We can do what the giants *can't* do — separate them." Nick swallowed. "If we can get to the center of the hydra where the knotting starts, we can hack it away. Like hitting a tree at its roots. I know it's crazy, but I think we can do it."

Laurie took his hand and gave it a single squeeze. "If we get out of this, I am going to be nice to you for a whole week."

"If we get out of this," Nick said, "you can

have any future bedroom of mine. Seriously."

"Now I know we're going to die," Laurie said, rolling her eyes.

They had to move fast, as two more giants had lumbered into view.

"Stick close to the trees," Laurie said. "The giants are coming from that way, so the sinkhole must be in the direction they're headed."

Nick and Laurie slunk close to the trees, letting the fight rage on behind them. When they found the sinkhole, the edges were slick with mud and the bottom was seething with fat dragons.

"Hold your breath," Nick said, and jumped. The dragons turned to bite at him. He waved Mallory's machete at them as he scrambled into the largest tunnel.

The hole was a tight fit, and as dirt crumbled down all around him, he imagined the walls closing in, the hole collapsing. He tried to take a deep breath, but he inhaled powdered soil and methane-thinned air. Tiny ants ran over his fingers and roots tangled in his hair. The passageway seemed to narrow as it veered downward.

He imagined Jared, Simon, and Mallory never getting up. He pictured Jules and Cindy unable to get away in time. He imagined the hydra moving toward Cindy's house, toward the place where his dad and Charlene waited. If he didn't stop the hydra—what would?

Forcing himself to crawl deeper into the tunnel, he looked at the handle of the machete in his hand. He remembered laughing at Laurie for paying attention to Noseeum Jack's giant-killing lessons. He remembered he was only good at video games, not at real life.

Where the tunnel dipped down lowest, the

methane got too thick to get a breath at all. He stopped.

Laurie touched his ankle. He jerked involuntarily, startled. "Ow," she said.

"Go back," he said, voice strained, and they both shuffled back until he could gulp air again. "You stay here."

"You can't go up there alone," said Laurie.

He couldn't see her expression in the dark. "There's only one machete. No point in you taking a risk. If I don't come back in ten minutes, get out of here."

"I'm not going to leave you," she said.

He thought he should argue, but at least she was waiting where it was mostly safe.

He forced himself onward.

Scuttling deeper, he forced himself onward until he could feel the tunnel curving upward. And then he was sucking in his breath and sticking his head up out of the hole.

He had expected to wait for the hydra to roll toward him, but it was right there. Its glistening bodies wove like water in the moonlight and for a moment Nick was too awed to move. He could see the knot of connective tissue that joined the dragons together, a mass of vines and clumps of no-longer-recognizable matter. He chopped hard, wildly. Black blood spattered his face. Above him he could hear screeching, and then his lungs ached and he dropped back down.

But when he tried to breathe, he couldn't. His head swam and he gasped. He felt hands drag him backward until suddenly there was air again.

"Aren't you glad I never listen to you?" asked Laurie.

"It didn't work," he managed to say. "Not enough air."

"It was a good plan," said Laurie.

"I just needed more time. I know I can do this. If I could just hold my breath longer—"

"Wait!" Laurie said. "The merfolk's cap! If it let you breathe underwater then maybe . . ."

"Maybe I could breathe in the tunnel." He rummaged through his pockets and pulled out the sea grass cap he'd gotten from the merfolk. It was worth a try.

He put it on his head and took back the machete.

Then he crawled back up through the hole.

He could breathe. He could worm his way through the tunnels, closer and closer to where the hydra writhed. He could come up nearly underneath it, climbing through its coils with the sea grass cap on his head and the machete in his hand.

Like he was some kind of hero.

Except this was nothing like playing a character in a video game.

He was terrified. He was dirty and he probably smelled awful. Sweat stung his eyes. There were no second chances or high scores or cheats that he could look up online.

This was real and awful, and he had no idea what he was doing but he was doing it anyway.

He cut into the middle of the hydra, chopping at the accumulated roots and dirt and filth that bound them together, chopping at the scales.

He chopped with all the grief in him, all the fear and the anger. All the things he'd sucked down and swallowed to make himself into someone who wouldn't bother anyone or bother with anything. He hacked up the dirt and the filth and the roots that held the dragons together like he was hacking apart every bit of his strained relationship with his dad, the loss of his mom, his fear of losing everyone all over again.

As the hydra moved, the dragons pulled apart, howling.

One knocked him to the ground. The machete nearly flew out of his hand, and he sprawled on his back. The dragon crawled over his body, its jaws close to his neck. Nick pressed the machete against its skin, but it bore down on him.

This was the end.

This was the end.

He thought about his mother and whether he would see her face, like he had when he was drowning. He hoped he would. He closed his eyes.

Then the weight was gone from his chest. He looked up in time to see a giant throwing one of the dragons against the dirt and then stomping on its back. Then flame exploded in the air in front of him.

All around him giants were closing in as the dragons moved chaotically, independently for the first time in centuries. Nick flattened himself against the wall of the sinkhole and watched as five hundred years of nature ripped itself apart.

The emergency room of the hospital was crowded with people as they all limped in, covered with mud. Nick's hair was singed, his skin felt sunburned, and he had a gash on his head, but he had never been happier. Laurie slumped into one of the waiting room chairs. She looked shaky, and both her knees were scraped up. A nurse brought a wheelchair for Jules. Jules got into it gingerly so he could elevate his leg. Cindy, whose parents had driven all of them over, immediately sat in his lap.

Nick guessed they weren't breaking up.

The Grace kids didn't look much better. Jared had a bruise over one eye. Simon had twisted his ankle, and it had swelled up so that his foot no longer quite fit in his shoe. Mallory had a gash on her cheek that she told them she hoped might heal to look like a dueling scar. All three of them seemed like they were about to fall asleep where they stood.

Jack Jr. was using a large plank of wood as

a walking stick. He leaned against the doorway, talking on a cell phone. When one of the nurses tried to get his information, he waved her off.

"Time for me to head out," he said when he hung up.

"Your leg looks really bad," Laurie said. "Don't you think you should get someone to check it?"

"I will," Jack Jr. said with a grin. "I think I should take myself and my sword out of here before someone sees me and starts to distrust lawyers more than ever. I just wanted to make sure you kids were safe. Dad wasn't happy we had to let some of the giants live, you know."

"Yeah," Nick said. "We *let them live*. That's one way to look at what happened."

"That's my dad for you." Jack Jr. shook his head. "He also wanted me to tell you that you were a bunch of real heroes, like in the old days."

"Really?" Laurie asked.

"Really," said Jack Jr. "And he's right."

"Nick's the hero," Mallory said, smiling. Nick could feel his cheeks get hot.

Jack reached into his coat, but this time he brought out nothing more than a business card. He placed it in Nick's hand. "Stay in touch."

He started toward the door, then turned back to tell Mallory to keep training. She promised she would.

They each got checked and bandaged in turn. Mallory called her dad. Jared taught them how to play gin rummy, which he'd learned from his aunt Lucy, and they played a few rounds before they realized that the hospital deck was missing a few cards.

"So, we're going back to Maine really soon," Simon said to Laurie.

"We can e-mail one another, though, right?" she asked.

"I'll e-mail you," he said, "but Jared's really bad at writing people back."

"I'd write *you* back," Jared said to Laurie.

Laurie smiled.

"Oh," said Mallory with a grin, leaning back in the waiting room chair, "I'm sure we'll all see each other again. Probably sooner than we think."

Nick saw something scuttle up to Laurie's leg. He was just about to try to whack it with his shoe when Sandspur leaped onto her lap.

She looked startled but began to pet him automatically.

"Is that your cat?" asked one of the nurses. "Pets aren't allowed in the hospital."

"I'll take him outside," said Laurie. She stood up.

"I'll go with you," said Nick.

They walked outside and sat on one of the benches under the overhang so they wouldn't get rained on. Nick wondered if Sandspur had made himself look like a cat or if the nurse had the Sight. The spriggan looked small and mostly harmless curled up on Laurie's lap. It was hard to imagine him swollen up so large that he could eat Nick.

"We can't keep him," Nick said.

"It doesn't matter," said Laurie. "It's not like you're going to live with us."

"I might. I mean, we might all live together again."

"Maybe we shouldn't," Laurie said, petting the spriggan. His three-toed feet twitched with pleasure.

Nick frowned. "What do you mean?"

"It's worse to have a dad and brothers and then lose them than not have them at all. If I'm going to lose you guys, then I just want to start getting used to it."

Nick took a deep breath. "Whatever happens with our parents, I will be your brother. Forever. I promise."

Laurie's face softened. "And I promise to be your sister." Laurie stuck out her pinkie, and they linked fingers to swear on it.

The rain ebbed as they watched the stream

of people go in and out of the emergency room. By the time Charlene and Nick's dad arrived, the mud had dried on Nick's skin, and he was trying without success to wipe his face on his shirt without making his face dirtier.

Charlene and Nick's dad walked close together, his dad's arm slung over Charlene's shoulder. They sprang apart when they saw the kids.

"We were so worried," Charlene said, sweeping Nick and Laurie into the same crushing hug.

"We're okay," Laurie said. "Jules is inside. He's okay too."

Nick's dad put his arm on Nick's shoulder awkwardly, then bent down to wrap his arms around Nick and Laurie and Charlene. "You're okay," he echoed. "I'm so glad you're all okay."

Charlene and Nick's dad signed a bunch of forms, and then the three kids were released. They said good-bye to Cindy and her parents, who seemed inclined to forgive everything, although they glowered at Jules when Cindy gave him a very lengthy parting hug. When Nick's family walked over to Jared, Simon, and Mallory, Nick saw that they were standing with their father. Mr. Grace was a tall, handsome man with oddly white teeth. He looked confused, but managed to shake everyone's hand anyway. They said more good-byes and made more promises of calling and e-mailing and seeing one another in places where there would be absolutely no faerie activity. Then Nick, Laurie, and Jules headed for the parking lot with Nick's dad and Laurie's mom. Charlene pushed Jules's wheelchair, although he insisted that he could walk with a crutch.

"I brought my car," Charlene said. "So, Laurie, I can take us back to the hotel and—"

"Um," Nick said, interrupting her, "I just wanted to say that I'm ready for change or whatever it was the counselor said. I want Laurie and Charlene to live with us. You know, in the future when we have a house."

"Me too," said Jules.

"Me three," said Laurie.

Dad looked at Charlene hopefully, and she smiled.

"I think we could do that," she said. "When we have a house."

"You do remember you promised me whatever bedroom I wanted, right?" Laurie said.

Nick groaned.

As they walked through the parking lot, Nick and Laurie lagged behind the others. The rain had stopped, and the sun was already high and bright in the sky. Nick blinked into the light.

"Look," said Laurie softly.

There, at the edge of the lot, was a single giant walking toward a copse of mangrove trees. As though it knew the kids were there, the giant turned to them, its stony face tranquil. Then it continued on its slow way into the wood.

Here ends
The Spiderwick
Chronicles

About TONY DiTERLIZZI . . .

Tony DiTerlizzi is the author and illustrator of *Jimmy Zangwow's Out-of-This-World Moon-Pie Adventure*, as well as the Zena Sutherland Award–winning *Ted*. In 2003, his brilliantly cinematic version of Mary Howitt's classic poem "The Spider and the Fly" received stellar reviews, earned Tony his second Zena Sutherland Award, and was honored as a Caldecott Honor Book. He followed that with the nonsense picture book *G Is for One Gzonk!* His recent novel, the *New York Times* bestseller *Kenny & the Dragon*, is his first chapter book. Tony's art has also graced the work of such well-known fantasy names as J. R. R. Tolkien, Anne McCaffrey, Peter S. Beagle, and Jane Yolen as well as Wizards of the Coast's *Magic: The Gathering*. He resides in Amherst, Massachusetts, with his wife and daughter. Visit Tony at diterlizzi.com.

and HOLLY BLACK

Holly Black's first novel, *Tithe: A Modern Faerie Tale*, was published in the fall of 2002. It was a YALSA Best Book for Young Adults and made YALSA's Teens' Top Ten booklist for 2003. A companion novel, *Valiant: A Modern Tale of Faerie*, won the Andre Norton Award for young adult fiction from the Science Fiction and Fantasy Writers of America. Her most recent solo venture is a *New York Times* bestselling companion to *Tithe* and *Valiant* entitled *Ironside: A Modern Faery's Tale*. She has also contributed to anthologies by Terri Windling, Ellen Datlow, and Tamora Pierce. Holly lives in Amherst, Massachusetts, with her husband, Theo, in a house with a secret library. Visit Holly at blackholly.com.

Thus ends the tales of Spiderwick.
A balance has been struck.
This peace between the worlds should last
(with any bit of luck).

Two cycles showed us wonders that
were closer than we thought
and evils which grew bigger than
the last one that was fought.

But through it all our heroes learned
a lesson from their plot:
That friends and family form a bond
which cuts through any knot.

It's time to close the book upon
these chronicles you've read.
But rest assured the faerie realm
is nowhere close to dead.

The world of the fantastical
has tales left still to share
of boggarts, nixies, sprites—those who
surround us everywhere.

The Grace kids and the Vargases
are not the only six
who'll have adventures magical
(and messes then to fix).

New stories need an author and
they'll need a hero, too.
So hone your senses, stay alert—
these tasks might fall to you.

Please keep a pen with you to write,
a pad, a brush, and ink.
Because *your* faerie tale just might . . .
start
SOONER
THAN YOU THINK!

ACKNOWLEDGMENTS

Tony and Holly would like to thank
Kevin, our faithful, fantastical guide
for this grand adventure;
Linda, for mapping out Mangrove Hollow
(and the spaghetti!);
Cassie, Cecil, Kelly, and Steve,
for their smarts;
Barry, for all his help;
Ellen, Julie, and all the folks at Gotham;
Scotty and Johnny Lind, for keeping the art on track;
Will and Joey B., for keeping Tony on track;
Theo, for all the patience and encouragement;
Angela (and Sophia) — more Spiderwick!
More endless nights of discussion!
At least it was on a beautiful, sunny Florida beach —

and all the wonderfully talented folks at S&S for
all of their support in bringing the last chapter
in the Spiderwick tale to life.

The text type for this book is set in Cochin.
The display types are set in Nevins Hand and Rackham.
The illustrations are rendered in pen and ink.
Managing editor: Dorothy Gribbin
Art director: Lizzy Bromley
Production manager: Chava Wolin

THE UNIVERSE IS FULL
OF MAGICAL THINGS
PATIENTLY WAITING
FOR OUR WITS
TO GROW SHARPER.

❧ ❧

—EDEN PHILLPOTTS,
A SHADOW PASSES (1918)

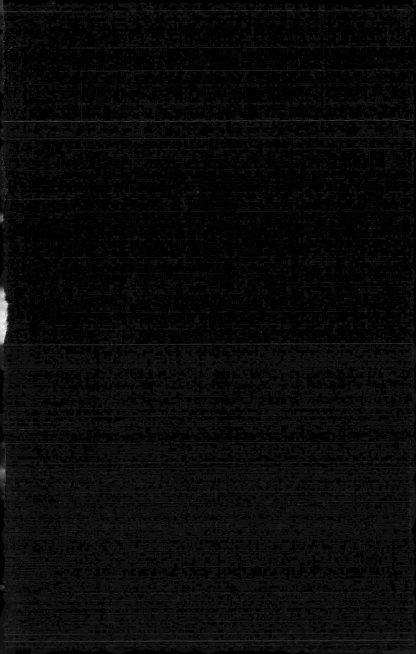